FIRST EDITION

Also by Thornton Sully

The Boy with a Torn Hat
The Courtesans of God

ALMOST AVALON

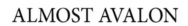

"Death and failure to those who
confuse love with desire ...
... but for those who get it right ... immortality
And a return to the garden."

Almost Avalon

A Novel by

THORNTON SULLY

A Word with You Press*
Publishers and Purveyors of Fine Stories in the Digital Age
310 East A Street, Suite B, Moscow, Idaho 83843

www.awordwithyoupress.com

Sully, Thornton
Almost Avalon

ISBN-10: 0988464624
ISBN-13: 978-0-9884646-2-9

Almost Avalon is published by:
A Word with You Press
310 East A Street, Suite B, Moscow, Idaho 83843

For information please direct emails to:
info@awordwithyoupress.com or visit our website:
www.awordwithyoupress.com

Book cover and interior design: Teri Rider, www.teririder.com

First edition, June 2015

Printed in the United States of America

10 9 8 7 6 5 4 3 2 1   15 16 17 18 19 20 21 22 23

Acknowledgments

It is here I acknowledge my extreme gratitude and unwavering love for my three children, Tesse, Tamara, and Morgan, without whom ink is nothing more than the secretion from a squid, and paper nothing more than reconstituted sawdust.

For Terri Fabrizio, whose impossible love
makes all things possible, *is why!*

I cast my net to a sea of indifference.
I drift, between the flow and ebb,
and I haul, from the sea of indifference,
the empty web.

Thornton Sully

— ONE —

December tumbled out of a storm cloud one night passing over the island on its way to Los Angeles. It *had* to have broken a few bones when it hit the deck, and it woke me, but I didn't crawl out from under the blankets to investigate. I was hoping maybe I dreamed it, but there it was, early the next morning, cold and wet, pounding on the aft hatch, hungry, and telling me how it liked its eggs. It made itself comfortable, with no sign of moving on. I've been looking over my shoulder for two weeks, and hiding the silverware since December made its descent. Tonight is no exception.

December. It is the bully of all months, the disciple of the twelve to betray the good intentions of the calendar. It does not roll off the tongue, like *April,* or *May.* It scrapes the roof of your mouth to speak its name. Its voice is brittle and its words are harsh, and it berates my every move. *You're going to lose her, you know. Go back, while you still can. I'll make it easy for you. She'll understand.*

When I answer, *You don't know who you're up against,* it says nothing, but sucks a degree or two out of the air when my back is turned.

My name is Aaron. I don't even know what I look like anymore, in case you're curious. I've got other priorities, but I'd like to think I'm at least half as handsome as Melissa is pretty. First words to her, from strangers, from men, are always about her looks, and she knows they do not speak of her beauty, but of their lust. I am the caretaker of her curse. But I am not drawn to the beauty, the perfect skin, the perfect face and form; I am drawn to the light within her. I am the keeper of her flame.

No ... I lie. I am drawn to her beauty like every other man who looks at her lips, and wonders, who by accident brushes against her hips, and imagines.

She tells her friends she's married to John Lennon. I'm a head taller than she is, and we're both a little too slim. Her hair is long, and dark, and straight; mine is a bit more complicated, and I'm probably overdue for a haircut. I might cave in to that the next time we pull around to Avalon to hit the Laundromat and take in a movie, but the beard is here to stay. When Neil Young sings "Twenty-four and there's so much more" we both know what he's talking about. I hope that helps.

I almost had this thing turned around; I was almost there. Traps baited and dropped from the face of Ribbon Rock all the way to the West End, after a week of downtime waiting for an alternator, after a week of flat and glassy water and watching other boats pull in each night fully loaded, and watching Melissa be everywhere but here. A few good days of fishing was all I needed on the lee side of bad weather, but then, December, and this storm.

I'd gone topside and groped my way forward to check the mooring, for chaffing and drift. Even tucked away where we were, the boat was bucking and doing its best to throw me, and the rain on the deck might as well have been bacon grease. Darkness had come by seven o'clock, and just got meaner, more serious, with each passing moment. The anchor light, small and dim atop the masthead, was fast asleep, and I was not about to let it nurse on the battery. The Gray Marine engine takes a big gulp to get itself started, and we needed to be out and working as soon as the weather broke.

One of the other lobster boats gave us a jump last week. It felt like a welfare check, or pity, and Melissa...I saw the way he looked at her, him thinking there was not enough of me to even bother to hide it. He mumbled a few words to her before flicking his cigarette in the water and powering off in his skiff. "You owe me," he said, over his shoulder.

I took a glance south of Cat Head and seaward. Nasty stuff, the night so wet and slippery most of the stars had lost their grip and slid off into the blackened sea, never to be seen again, after the brief sizzle as they lost their fire. Even the moon would have nothing to do with this storm, and had gone off to some bar to wait it out, leaving a bullet hole in the sky that gushed wind and blackness and blood. I did my work by the blink of lightning, and when I was done, I worked my way aft. I looked through the port hole in the door to the cabin. Melissa had just lit the alcohol stove. I rapped twice on the wood to let her brace herself before I slid the door open and dropped below.

I shrugged off my pea coat, and eased it between the third and top step of the companionway, thinking maybe it would drip itself dry if it had nothing better to do. I dusted excess moisture from my watch-cap before setting it on the mahogany chart table.

Melissa pumped a few spurts of water into the kettle and set it on the stove, flattening the blue flame. When she turned my way I slipped my finger into the loop on her jeans where there should have been a belt coiled around her, but we needed the belt to cinch a split in the oar of the dinghy. I pulled her to me. I almost touched her recent wound.

It happened like this: The storm had been rolling our way a few days ago—you could feel it in the water, but not yet in the air— when kelp snagged the last trap of the day. As it was topping the gun'll, the line snapped, just as Melissa was coming to me with a cup of coffee. The welts on her torso? The signature of my neglect. The burn to her fingers as the coffee tumbled? The nuance of my affection for her. I did that to her. That line should have been replaced a month ago.

I was contagious with rain and made slick her only dry shirt. I should have known better, but I selfishly wanted that re-assurance a man gets when woman parts are firmly up against him, especially a woman he loves. She backed off and put her hand to her breast, then looked in disbelief at her fingers, and then at me. She was moist with colorless blood, evidence she had been wounded, pierced—again by my own hand. She said nothing, and wiped her hand on her jeans. I have punctured her heart and now there is nothing left to do but gamble for her clothes.

I knelt before her, as I did every night of rain, hoping to be knighted. *Arise, Sir Aaron.* But she never said those words. Instead, while I supplicated, she tugged my armor of wool over my shoulders and bunched it into the small sink, keeping it at arm's length.

I hoisted myself from the floorboards, and eased in to the settee, fisting and opening my icy hands to pump some blood into them and get them back on board. Eight o'clock was approaching, and I needed them dressed and sober. Someday, perhaps, by some noble act, she will see her way clear to knight me.

I tested my fingers, drumming them a bit on the side of the radio bolted squarely to the table where it joined the hull, and as I turned it on, its red light glowed like the beacon light on a jetty, somewhere on that mahogany shore. But for a burning candle, and the low blue flame of the alcohol stove, it was the only illumination from within the cabin. That, and the constant halo that blinds me whenever Melissa looks my way. *Jesus*, she says, *I'm not an angel*, as she preens the feathers of her wings.

My hands were obedient but still unfeeling. Or is that my heart? One hand rotated the dial and tuned the radio. The other one stood watch. I cranked up the volume as high as it could go, just as December dumped another bucket of marbles on the roof, and the sky cleared its throat of thunder. My marine-band was navy surplus, but reception on the windward side of the island was always dicey.

We were bobbing up and down and confusing the hell out of the radio waves coming out of San Pedro. The boat shifted on its mooring yet another time, as faintly, sandpapered with static, the Eight O'clock Notice to Mariners commenced. "Catalina Island... wind out of the southwest...twenty-five to thirty knots..." the voice babbled like a coughing Pentecostal. "...six to eight foot swells at ten second intervals."

The voice was so distant that it made it hard to believe that the mainland was less than the twenty-minute freeway drive from Carlsbad to San Diego. The impartial, detached voice that I couldn't believe belonged to someone with a pulse continued, "...currently raining...visibility two miles with low clouds and fog...estimaxxxx..."

"Jesus! Can you believe this!" Just when I'd dialed in a fix an errant gust of wind spat at us crude and rude from out of the Northeast, shifting the boat, changing *everything.* If the battery had been stronger, or my fingers more nimble, I could have, I *know* I could have picked it up. I grit my teeth and threatened my fingers. They trembled and felt my wrath. They have seen what I do to an abalone with a knife when I bait my traps.

The radio continued to screech and wail, but I missed the *forecast,* the only thing that mattered. I put the radio out of its raspy misery with a flip of the toggle-switch. The bubble of red light faded to darkness as a beacon burns out, smoldering for a moment in the dim darkness, its passion spent.

"I'm sorry." I leaned my head back against the bulkhead.

"It's not your fault."

"I mean...losing my temper."

She took my hand. "It's all right," Melissa said. "My guess is we're not going anywhere in the morning." The water for tea was not yet at boil, and she sat across from me for a moment, until the kettle screamed.

We've been breathing the same air, over and over again, for quite some time, now, and it tastes like wet cardboard. Maybe tea can change the taste in my mouth.

San Pedro's Ordinary Seaman didn't get it right.

I have more faith in an old gull, gray and huddled for the last two days between two salvaged lobster traps on deck. I trust his intelligence. In his wings: the weather recorded, and within his dulled eyes: a forecast.

The sweater in the sink had not been dry for three days and had not seen the sun in twice that long. Faded wool, and heavy with water. I believe that in its youth, maybe even as late as last summer, it was peach colored. It's the color of oatmeal now, which is to say, no color at all. But, in spite of its dampness, it locked out the wind the same ironic way a deck swollen with water stays water-tight. I crawled inside it once more, compelled into action by the slap of water on the hull, the shrill cry of the wind as it slit its tongue on the stays of the mooring mast, and the rockslide of rain on the roof.

"This seems to be picking up. I'm going out to take another look at the mooring. See how we're holding."

"Pick up the Sunday paper while you're out, won't you?"

"Sure."

Melissa knew the drill. Opening the hatch put the candle at risk. The wind was as hungry as we were, and had sharper teeth. We'd seen it tear a chunk of air out of our little cave swift as a shark and disappear into deep water. We'd seen it swallow the flame whole before, on other nights like this, and from this, we learned.

I slipped back into the pea coat, slipped on my watch cap, and turned to see that Melissa had canopied herself over the candle.

"Got it," she said. The flame clung to the wick as if it were the last petal of a flower. She loves me … she loves me not … she …

I opened the hatch and stepped up and out on the deck. Less than a year ago we'd be flipping TV channels about this time, or *raiding* the refrigerator during a commercial break. Stuff so tame you trick yourself into thinking life is an adventure by saying that getting off the sofa to paw through left-overs for cold pizza in the fridge is a *raid*.

I looked skyward. This broken canopy that is falling upon me, is *this* what Melissa wants? The safe and numbing drama of the CBS Evening News with Walter Cronkite; is *that* what she wanted?

I wasn't on deck more than a moment when I heard a voice. *Join me, won't you?* offered the night. *Let me carry you away with me, as I do the wind, to join the decomposed and just drift off into the sweet darkness. Wouldn't you like that?* It required only that I nod in consent. But how can I drift? There is a woman down below who loves me, and she's counting on me. I can fail myself, I have failed myself, but I can never fail her. *We'll have this talk again,* said the night, *but wasn't there some purpose to you stepping out here, in the cold?*

The mooring, yes, that umbilical cord that keeps us tethered to this womb of a harbor. That is what I'm here for. Confined, and unable to fish, checking the mooring while braving bullets of rain was the only manly act of self-sacrifice left me. And for a moment, I escape Melissa's scrutiny, and can stand erect and without shame. I have no need of dignity in the dark, where there is no witness to any act, noble or foul.

The trek against the wind to the bow was of course unnecessary, the boat being just as secure now as it was a half an hour ago. Somebody from Marina Del Rey paid three hundred fifty dollars for this mooring, for the one summer weekend or two that they would motor over, when the water was so flat and the wind so nothing at all a Danforth could have held them.

The Catalina Island Company that ran the place kept an elephant graveyard of engines died of cardiac arrest, pistons frozen in the arteries so hard by rust they were *Do Not Resuscitate.* They laced half inch chain through the engine blocks, sunk them in a line with a buoy and a number. They didn't budge, except maybe to burrow into the sand. We've never dragged but sometimes I play out a little more line if it's chaffing through the chocks.

I scanned the horizon for a break in the storm, but the mouth of the harbor was black as blood, and I saw only the lights from the few other fishing boats bouncing like drunken fire-flies. It was a mistake to have wasted the power from the twelve-volt on a weather report that told me nothing that I did not already know. I would like to have heard if the storm was changing direction, though. That would have been helpful. Even if it were raining just as hard in the morning I could pull if the wind changed direction and started to beat down the swells. If the wind died, fishing in two days. But if it changed direction, tonight, right now, I could fish in the morning. It had only to change direction.

As things were, the swells were not tickling their way down the coast as they usually do, casual as tourists, but were getting backlogged and blue-balled bulking up directly on the face of the cliffs, and punching it out, making an approach to the traps death by stupidity. A smaller boat, maybe, but not mine. Even in good weather it was a hard boat to maneuver near the rocks. It was a soft-chine Monterey boat, too big and with too much roll to fish lobsters, but it had headroom, a vee-berth up forward, a galley and head, a settee and even a hanging locker. We couldn't get that in a skiff with a cuddy cabin, not even a Radon boat.

It was, by default, a lobster boat.

The sky and sea sloshed together like bilge oil, too dark and heavy to even tell where the island ended and open water began. Another sporadic pulse of lightning lit up the sea, and the sea was ugly. I could make out a lot of kelp drifting by the boat at a good clip towards the beach, telling me that bad water at the harbor entrance was bound to seal us in a few days more.

In the darkness, the bow of the boat becomes my confessional, and here I confess my sins, then cut them loose. They get a little more distant from me, drift off across the water and disappear. It's easy, and gets easier. I numb myself to my own imperfections. But to confess love for another being, for a woman? I tremble. I hear the sharp smack of a gavel, and remind myself it is only thunder. I am as angry as a man freshly in love, with suddenly so much to conceal, so much to make disappear for his beloved. It is this, the night, my confessor, extracts from me, and this does not easily drift away with the current ...

... The wind must be reasonable. It *has* to change direction. In the distance there is a flash of gunfire. I hear a fresh volley of rain tearing through the darkness and heading my way.

I brace myself.

I can feel it coming.

Without flinching I check the mooring line and bitt.

I decline the blindfold and cigarette as the rain crosses the bow.

Melissa, forgive me. I only slept with that woman because ...

... I was riddled by gunfire, my confession incomplete.

—⁓— TWO —⁓—

"Hey, why you keep checking it? We seem to be holding just fine."

I shrugged out of my gear without her help, the coat on the steps, the sweater in the sink. I sat down before I answered her, "But, in this weather ..." and then I realized there was no answer, the nobility of my act a work of fiction.

I was only vaguely aware that Melissa had pulled off my boots. She then took my hands and wrapped them around a warm cup from which vaporized the faint scent of green tea.

She sat across from me, and leaned back to let me drink, watching me. I couldn't think of anything else to lie to her about. Is it really her on the other side of the vapor, being so kind?

I closed my eyes and steam anointed my brow. I set the cup down, still warming my hands by it, and I, too, leaned back, feeling released by the warmth as the tea channeled its way into me. When the steam on my brow cooled, I opened my eyes, and there it was, that smile of hers, that's got me doing all this.

Melissa reached under her seat and pulled out her journal, wrapped in a towel like baby swaddling and sheathed in a plastic Woolworth's bag. Her one true pleasure that even December could not usurp. She un-scrolled the aluminum foil in which were a few pens and colored pencils, and she began to write. I could not read the upside-down words as they drifted upon the page as I was across from her, nor would I choose to read them. They were hers, to do with as she liked. But I could make out, in the margins, and sometimes dividing one passage from another, her sweet little drawings; a starfish, a whale, sunflowers, or a blackbird testing its wings.

Melissa winced as a drop of rainwater could hold on no longer and fell from the ceiling, pelting her on the back of the neck. She placed a pan under what apparently was the newest point of siege, and water began slowly to collect itself. "That's *our* roof leakin'," she said. "Beats paying rent for one that leaks just as bad."

Our apartment in Encinitas never leaked a drop. And, anyway, it never rains in Southern California, Catalina excepted. Still, it sounded good, coming from her. I lie to distance myself from reality. Melissa lies to create a better reality.

But the truth was, we were just overwhelmed by the rain, cold and copious thing that it had become. No corner of the boat was ever dry. Even our words were made of water. To speak them was to wring them out of a wash-rag, spilling them on the table, spilling them on to one another each time we spoke. Of late, we say very little to each other, and what we speak travels no faster than the Monterey boat, slow and sluggish between trough and crest.

It was with words unspoken, then, that I thought of repairs for the boat.

A few good days of fishing would make such a difference, just a few good days.

"The storm should get the lobsters moving," I said. "That's what the other boats tell me. They always pull well after a storm."

Melissa held up her hand without looking up from her journal and kept writing; I had interrupted a thought in mid-sentence.

I waited for her to lift her head to look at me. But that damned journal, which I praise.

There I posed, the centerfold of despair, staring out the window, watching the rain dilute a hemlock sea, watching it as the boat contorted at the end of the mooring line, like an animal struggling with its foot in a trap, hearing the hunter approach.

We tried to imagine what it would be like, when we were living at the mainland, but our understanding of the weather then was as mindless as the voice on the radio an hour before. Never did I say "There is so much rain" without a tremor of disbelief, and while there was that trace, while I pretended to be shocked by what was happening, I could somehow avoid apologizing for it, for inviting her into all this.

It had been about eight months since I had taken her from the mainland. The summer was easy. I worked in the boat yard, and Melissa as a waitress in the café. We lived on the boat, sometimes sleeping on the deck under the stars, and waited for October and the start of lobster season. Laid off after Labor Day, as we knew we would be, September was a month with nothing to do, and we did *nothing*, very, very well. A month to camp in the interior of the island, which can look like Vermont in the fall, a month to snorkel for abalone and spear fish, a month for Melissa to sit alone in the hills and oversee the world, journal in hand. A month of making love on secluded beaches; a month of making amends.

Catalina! Twenty or thirty miles at most from Los Angeles, an island, one of the Channel Islands, grazing in the blue-grass of the Pacific like indifferent sheep or goats. The windward side of the island was stark, striking, erodible and eroded, but it was redeemed by the presence of an all-weather harbor that bore the same name as the island itself, and the cliffs surrendered themselves to the gentle sloping at the Isthmus, and with the first rains of late fall, all was green.

Years ago a small herd of buffalo were barged over for a John Wayne movie. Their descendants meander on the hillsides and in the trough of the Isthmus. They mingle with goats and tourists and crop the tall grass that ripples like the water on the horizon when the sun plunges to cool itself at the end of the day ... .

... My skin was brown and my hair was bleached, just a few short months ago ... .

Melissa folded her journal, and before she thought about what to do next she pulled out a deck of cards from a canister lodged between the sweat sheathing and the hull. All forty-eight or fifty of them were warped by moisture and worn beyond retirement. She dealt the first hand. The three of hearts was torn slightly down the middle, a spattering of wax stained the black queen, and the six of clubs was dog-eared. Marks on half a dozen other cards made them readable from either side, but we overlooked that and played. This was the surrogate for the adventures that I had promised her, and even believed I could deliver.

Ours had been the dream that everyone dreams who reads Treasure Island. Magnificent square-rigged schooners, tall and proud, with sails as full as the love Melissa and I had for one another, coming over the horizon and dropping anchor, dropping sails. But the vessels that round Cat Head now stagger in drunk, smelling of Diesel and larceny— degenerated fishing boats, lean and un-kept like those who manned them. It was hard to find a boat without a gun on board, "to pop the goats on the cliffs," they said, to tumble down to the water to cook in charcoal on the transom of a boat, but I have seen also bull seals bloated and floating and freckled with buckshot, have seen gulls taken down like clay pigeons, for alcohol inspired sport.

Our pirates, the lobster fishermen, would drink coffee together in the harbor each morning, almost like a family, but when the fishing was bad, as it often was, they would steal from each other once they rounded Cat Head, the prominent point that sentried the harbor. And then in the evening, it was all bluff, bluff and beer, as they rafted together for their evening pissing contest.

We never rafted with them; I was the only one with a woman on board. They thought it so unfair that someone like me should have someone like her. They were real men. Dirt under the fingernails and sweat pasting their wife-beater shirts in place. Beer on their breath like a bird on a branch. What was her problem?

After a while, I noticed that I had a pile of matchsticks on my side of the table, and that Melissa had very few. The isolation, the boredom, was a blunt and scar-less beating that I never saw coming. We just need to ride it out.

There was escape, I suppose, if we really wanted it. We've got a dinghy trailing off the stern. The wind would have been with us if we wanted to row in, to row ashore to the settlement. A juke box, a pool table, a bar, and the skeleton crew that anchored the island and kept it from drifting out to sea until next summer. But the wind would be against us rowing back, and it would have been too much to contend with, and the rain would have us flirting with pneumonia.

As I scraped minutes from the cliffs of time, I was looking less and less at my benevolent Medusa, and I became less able to distract myself with a game of cards. The lapping and the rocking would not relent, the bobbing up and down, the collage of rain and salt and lights smeared on the porthole like butter, an animated finger painting. Melissa had dealt the last four hands, I think. I was staring through the glass. I was looking around the perimeter of the overhead that wept here and there with rain. I was staring down the radio. I was looking at the candle. I was looking everywhere but into the eyes of my beloved, for I would surely turn to stone if within that sweet deepness I should see what I have done to her.

Thank god the deck above us was cambered. Most of the water that worked its way in would slither, rat-like, down the corners of the cabin, but for the few brave or suicidal droplets that took direct aim and dove for our shoulders or neck, free fall to the jugular.

Distracted, again, I was, by a drop of rain, dripping down, spiraling down my chest. Melissa was no longer across from me. Her fingers were dripping downward, weaving in and out of the buttons of my shirt. My clothes, almost dry. My skin, warm underneath my flannel shirt.

"I have some very nice things to say to your body," she said, "but your clothes keep interrupting me."

I closed my eyes, before I turned to stone.

—ⱳⱳ— THREE —ⱳⱳ—

I pulled myself from a counterfeit sleep, pulled myself up like an empty trap. It was still dark, and in the darkness Melissa's body was a silhouette of Catalina on a supple night when approached by sea, when the features are so soft as to be indistinct, but discernible from the sky by the intensity of its hue. A boat, overloaded with a long day, if not with fish, swollen in desire for an island and an anchorage, and the island, inviting the boat like my father luring me home with promises of sobriety; such was Catalina at night, and able to soothe me.

Sometimes we come in with supplies from San Pedro, and return to Catalina by night, and the island reminds me of Melissa, sleeping. But now I think of how beautiful and dark the island can be, and for a moment I think of summer, the one past, and the one to come, as silence pulsates from the island, a heartbeat. Like a beacon, am I drawn to this woman. This island is magnetic north, and I return, but Melissa is true north, and I follow.

It seemed every bit as lightless as when I had blown out the candle. There was not sleep; there was the insane ritual of checking the mooring line. Gentle as her sleep, I slipped from the berth, till my hand was no longer a part of the silhouette, and I drew closed the curtain that separated the berth from the cabin. My hands Brailed their way across the table and discovered a crate of matches, the alphabet of fire and light.

I struck one match, and its flame was harsh and abrupt to my newly opened eyes, but as the match found the wick of the candle, the candle began to bud, hollowing out a space in the darkness and tapering like the spire of a church. On every window was the reflection of the flame, pained and gentle, the face of Christ on a wash woman's cleaning rag.

My clothes were listless on the table. I would dress myself after I secured the mooring. I knew I would not be returning to my bunk, too restless for that, and I wanted something dry when I came below. Fair trade for wet electricity of cold that awaited me on deck.

Almost to my disappointment, I found that the mooring was secure. The hemp had not chafed in the least. It might have been different if the wind were more southerly, but under any conditions, Cat Harbor was the most secure anchorage on the island.

This time there was no surveillance of the horizon for a break in the codeine-colored sky. It was all made very clear to me upon my bare shoulders and back, as I flinched and made my way back to the cabin.

I grasped the latch. I paused a moment for a wind gust to pass, and in one movement I slid open the hatch and lowered myself, bypassing the four steps. The candle was flickering precariously, and I pivoted to get the hatch closed, but before I could close it I saw the empty spot between the two lobster traps on the stern deck.

I closed the hatch and rubbed the port clean and looked once again. The gull was gone.

I'd grown fond of it. I pulled my hair behind my head as I stood there. I swore with my head slumped reverently. That was to be the gull's only eulogy.

Though it had been with us only a couple of days, he trusted me to take pancakes from my hand, as he was healing from whatever the storm or aging had done to him. I was thinking of giving it a name.

A shiver alerted me to my nakedness. I pulled clothes over my body. The table was clear now, except for the candle and the radio at one end. I looked around the cabin from the corner where I sat and tried to invent things to help pass what remained of the night. Why could I not sleep? I remember when I had made the ten hour voyage from Oceanside to Cat Harbor, not putting out until four in the afternoon. Ten hours at the wheel. I could so easily have slept then. I had wanted it so badly, so desperately, and it was only the distance from the boat to the harbor that kept me from sleeping. I had almost collapsed at the wheel, then I was so willing.

Melissa sleeps. God, I was grateful that she was sleeping. She was safe, a refugee from the wars of wakefulness.

A mild shift in the wind rocked the boat slightly, and I could hear water sloshing n the bilge.

I stumbled to the pump, thankful for the water in the bilge that gave me something to do. I choked the handle of the pump, but the scraping of the plunger in the shaft, the regurgitating water, too loud and grotesque. After two or three strokes, I let it be, and hesitated to breathe, to hear if Melissa stirred. I pulled myself to the table. Did I evict her from the sanctuary of sleep?

She accuses me sometimes I know, of giving to get. She doubts me, but it's not that way. And she gets me scared to do things for her, too, that way. But this time, she won't even know that I swallowed another little dose of monotony so that she could sleep.

The thought came, that maybe I am the person she thinks I am, kind and generous. Almost at once I felt something heavy rolling into my body. I knew what it was and I blew out the candle. I laid my head on the table.

──〜── FOUR ──〜──

I was dreaming of the gull when I ran out of sleep. The wind had changed. The Monterey pointed, but the dinghy was filled to the rails with rain and was sluggish, and struck bluntly amidships before drifting to its rightful place off the stern.

My shoulders and neck stiffened as I prepared to be pelted by rain when I opened the hatch and lurched out on deck. But the rain had stopped? Of course. That's right. The drumming on the cabin had stopped.

The air looked and tasted gray, as the darkness slipped into deep water, beneath paddies of kelp that began collecting in the harbor, dislodged by the storm. One of the oars had been blown out of the dinghy. Most likely it would be on shore, but the wind and the tide were changing, and if it wasn't already on the beach, it would be on its way to Hawaii.

I went below for a coffee can, knowing it would be almost empty, to use to bail the dinghy. I opened the food locker over the table, and it was then that I discovered the most severe damage of the storm. The rain had leaked in and disintegrated the paper bag that held a half a dozen eggs. Broken shells littered the shelf like driftwood on the shore and were bleeding gold and silver. It must have happened as the boat shifted. I didn't hear it, the sound of eggs colliding into one another muffled by the dinghy bashing the hull.

The sack of instant pancake mix was paste. I felt the loaf of bread, a sponge, but as I hauled it out, a solitary egg that was wedged behind it wobbled my way and off the shelf. I caught the sole survivor with my free hand, put it in my watch-cap to keep it from rolling and set it where the bread had been.

I turned to assure myself that Melissa was not up, and did not see this. The wind, once again, changed its mind and direction, and again the shore boat was punching at the rub rail. I knew the consequences if I hesitated any longer—Melissa would be awakened.

I reached for the coffee can, shook it once. Completely empty. Strange, I was almost thankful for that. Made it simple. I mopped the broken eggs into the coffee can, using the loaf of bread like a rag.

I stepped out on deck, shook the can and slipped everything over the side—the pancake mix, the eggs and bread. Somebody should say a few words.

The intensity of the two hulls colliding quickened me. Melissa must be exhausted, I thought, to be sleeping through this. I was barefoot. I rolled up my pants and lowered myself into the dinghy and began bailing.

I saw streaks of white across the mouth of the harbor and I began to doubt if even a change in the wind was going to help.

I was thinking about Melissa, and I was thinking about my traps, as I finished bailing. I had seen the other boats move their traps into deeper water before the storm, and I did the same, but I wasn't certain if I had put them in deep enough water to survive whatever punishment the swells might give. Melissa? How deep is the water beneath us?

I would have to tell her about the food, before she found out on her own. I somehow thought if I sat below at the table I would figure out what to say, but when I came below Melissa was already up, with a blanket draped over her shoulders. She was just boiling some water, and, anticipating her next move, I sat down strategically between her and the food locker.

"We're out of coffee," I said. "How long you been up?"

"Not long."

"It stopped raining."

"Yeah, I know." She leaned over to reach the food locker. I intercepted her hand, and pulled it to me, to my shoulder. She nestled there for a moment, half with affection, but half with sleep and weariness. I could feel her weight and I knew she was tired.

I was wondering what I would do when she reached for the locker again, but was given a mild reprieve, for she hoisted herself and turned to the stove, and said "Well, I prefer tea in the morning, anyway."

The tea had been left—miraculously—over the stove, and was dry. She yawned, making her lie credible by her seeming indifference.

"Why don't you go back to bed? You look so tired."

"Too tired to sleep." Two lies in a row. "Anyway, the stove's on, and I'm gonna fix you breakfast."

"Actually, I'm not that hungry. I guess it's the weather."

"No, really, you'll need your strength to fish. Maybe some pancakes?"

I looked out the window from my place at the corner, and now with the light of morning, could see that the sky was getting heavy again. I doubted that I would be fishing that day.

"I guess you're right," I said, "but maybe later on. I'm quite serious, though, about you lying down. Tell you what, try to sleep for another hour and I'll wake you with a soft boiled egg, or something."

She smiled somberly, "O.K." she said, "but only one egg. I want … only one egg." Her eyes turned awkwardly from me as she said it. I slurred, and said nothing.

She knows!

I felt the blood draining from my face, and like spindrift announces a storm, the flush feeling that was overtaking me told me that in a moment, I would be crying; I would be unmanly when manliness from me was what she most needed. Oh no! She knows! In a hastily gathered breath, the way I used to pack my bags and run off, sometimes, like that, I said, I slurred, "Well, I think I'll wait topside," and I spun from the table before she could make a reply or see my face. I grabbed the latch. Swollen tight! Melissa caught me by the sweater.

She said something but for the life of me I don't know what it was, she was so weak, whimpering. I knew she was crying, too. I turned around, saw her huddled in the blanket, holding my watch cap in her outstretched hand.

Almost bleeding, from my mouth flowed the words, "I'm so sorry," and there was almost no strength to say even that. She dropped the empty watch cap on the table, and we collapsed into each other, and the blanket would have fallen, would have fallen, but I held it around her shoulders, pulled her into my dry sweater. "I'm so sorry," I said, and the most gracious fingers that have ever touched me closed my lips as I was about to say it for a third time. Her hand, I kissed it.

Cautiously, we withdraw from each other and sat down at our places. I looked directly into her. So this is the shape of a final moment. "My god, you're so lovely," I said.

She smiled, and I was filled.

After some time, I began, "I really want you to have the egg."

"I don't want it. I mean, I can't, not like this, not if it means that you're not gonna eat."

"The pancake stuff got wet, too." She took the hit with grace and dignity.

I was staring out the window, and I could see the mouth of the harbor. "It just might break today," I said lightly. "Look, if we have to, I can sell the traps on the stern … Please … take the last egg. I don't want it."

"But neither do I."

"Do you let me do nothing for you?" I pleaded.

I wondered how many traps I had lost in the storm. One week of good pulls would make such a difference. I hope she says nothing. One week of good fishing.

"I ate last night, and besides, I don't think you slept at all. Let me fry you the egg."

The cabin was so small that I could not have drifted into another room, but somehow, right before her very eyes, I vanished. When I reappeared, Melissa was fully dressed, and handing me a cup of tea, as she had done the night before.

Awake now, and completely alert, as if she had not lost weight, as if she were not wanting of sleep, she asked again, "Let me fry you the egg?"

I smiled, blushed a bit, and I made certain that she knew that the smile was directed towards her, and that I was not just amused. She was magnificent, and I had no choice but to shake my head lightly, "No."

"Well then," she said, "It looks like we're going to feed the gull again this morning. Let's see if he's up."

It wasn't extortion, it wasn't! She thought it would please me to see the gull fed. She had seen my affection for the bird. She reached for the latch.

"Wait a minute."

She turned my way.

"Don't we have some powdered milk left over the stove? I'll bet it's dry. We can mix it with the egg, have it scrambled." I couldn't let her find out about the gull.

"But you *detest* your eggs scrambled with that god-awful powdered milk."

"No, I don't. I love it that way. Just like you like green tea instead of coffee." I wasn't sure she'd go for it.

She put her hand on my cheek, and, fearful that she might draw it away a moment too soon, I held it in place. "All right," she said.

This is what love looks like, I thought. A little seal pup, playful, sweet, harmless and curious, that suddenly pokes his head up from the soft water near the boat and gives you just a glimpse of himself, before he swims off. I would tell her about the gull, but that could wait.

"Hold this," she said. Melissa pulled down what remained of the carton of powdered milk. Yes, still dry. I studied the egg in the palm of my hand. It is fragile, like Melissa … . No, that's not right. It is fragile, like me.

She turned to me, lifting the egg from my palm. Melissa has such lovely hands. They flutter like birds, sometimes, when she speaks. Do real men see that? She gave me a spoon for my tea. She turned to the stove, and I'm sure she heard me strike a match. She looked back at me once briefly, and smiled, knowing that I was lighting the candle, and the grayness inside the cabin disappeared. I was stirring my tea. It's really not so bad, green tea. "Melissa, the only man in your life who could love you more than me is the man you are helping me to become." The spoon, ringing in my cup, so lovely.

But in what seemed to start the argument all over again, she said, "Care for yours sunny side up, Babe?" She was beginning to choke with tears, I could hear her.

Slowly, using the table to hoist myself, I stood and stepped behind her. I put my arms around her waist, and my cheek upon her shoulder, comforting and taking comfort. She was trembling, and I did not understand. I did not understand until of course, I looked down over her shoulder. There, in the dish, I saw the egg.

It had a double yoke.

—ᴡᴡ— FIVE —ᴡᴡ—

The gull.

Melissa did not understand why the search for the oar had been so cursory. We had just barely been on shore. I had been strolling twenty yards to her side, and stopped at seeing a thick tangle of kelp that was attracting an unusual number of flies. I paused, looked down the strand, and then to Melissa, and simply declared that the oar had been washed out to sea. As I started walking down the road, I turned my head once to the place where I had stopped, but said nothing.

On the way into Avalon, in the back of a delivery truck, I remarked that the oars were rather worn down by the locks and probably would have needed to be replaced in a month or two anyway.

It had been an appropriate day for going into town. The sky eventually had been cleansed of its excesses, both rain and wind, but the water was still rough. We couldn't fish. It was different for the other fishermen with the smaller boats that could somehow hang in between the swells and pull out in a hurry, but it was clear that it was too rough for me and my boat, too much strain and working every moment just to keep off the rocks. I bent a prop once on a wash rock, limped home until I could pull it. It could just as well have been a plank and we'd have been under. It's not holding up bad for a boat so old, but it is old and it pulls a lot of water with it these days.

Anyway, the bad water made the decision not to fish, not I. It made going into town an easy thing.

Johnny, who had one green eye and one blue, made the runs for the Island Company. It was against company policy to take passengers when he went to Avalon, but we waited over a hill about a quarter mile from the settlement, and it was there he picked us up and dropped us off, and nobody was the wiser.

There would come a time, I knew, when even if the water were perfect and the sky clear, and everything functional on the boat, still we would take the liberty to go into town. We would not have to time that to bad weather or water. We would go into town and our day would be planned over breakfast at the Prego. I imagined commenting with a bit of reserve that the food had been good, but not extraordinary, that yes, Melissa, you are certainly a better cook. I imagined saying "Keep the change." We would go to the movies, feed the pigeons, or watch the people from the pier who came in on the shore boats. It would be a perfect day, the one I imagined, a day that could have brought in full traps, a day that fishermen do not believe can happen, but I would turn my back to it, like a matador turns his back to his bull.

It would take just a few days of fishing to give me that.

We sculled our way back to the boat. Sacks of groceries. I wondered if it would have been enough to sell just one trap. It didn't matter. After a bit of good fishing, I could replace the old rusted traps with new ones, and the fisherman who bought my traps that morning would think that I sold them because I had intended to replace them with new ones.

That's what I told him, anyway. He did not really care. It gave him a chance to peel money from a hefty wad of twenties in front of Melissa, and stuff it back in his pocket.

That day, like the weather, had passed with indifference, but now we had a bit of food, and the food anchored us securely to the night, and we were not restless.

From its lee shore origins, the morning fog came charging over the hill and on through the Isthmus, galloping down to the beach like a confederate army. It was one mass of rioting grayness, silent only to the ear, and its penetration was no less horrifying than cannon and shot.

The beach became a battlefront, for a current of air from the windward side had engaged the fog there, to resolve the question of territory and of dominance. We cowered in our boat, aware of its relative safety. Eventually, I slid open the hatch, and, exposing no more of myself than I had to, I peered into the morning.

There was an after-battle stillness. The fog had receded and the tide had retreated, but gulls still huddled in some obscure part of the harbor, riding out their inadequacies like monks in a monastery.

Timidly, the sun appeared. Scattered on the shoreline on the beach was a disarray of driftwood, abandoned rifles and dismantled cannons. Flies were attacking corpses of rotting kelp, which sloshed listlessly in the shallows. The sun that appeared was round. I expected almost to see it fragmented or missing a few pieces, but it had survived, intact and unscathed. It was paler than I had remembered it from a few days earlier, almost a week earlier, when I had last seen it, when it had eaten of the blue sky, which is its bread.

"I think it's over," I whispered to Melissa. "We fish today."

The gulls, revived by a few inhalations of warm sunlight sensed it too, sensed that it was time to fish. It was easy for them to fish after a storm. Much kelp is broken and drifting, and the kelp attracts the small fish. The gulls would find a paddy of kelp, float with it and rest, and simply wait.

It was never like that if there had been no storm. Then the fishing drained them, for they would have to fly, and hunt, and strain, and dive on shadows, but after a storm it was always easy. They could drift with the kelp, and the sun would mend them, and the small fish would come right up to the surface under them. Strangely, the kelp never breaks up before the birds are strong. Then, as gradually as the storm is sudden or can be sudden, and as rhythmically as birth, the kelp unweaves itself and the gulls become true and virtuous fishermen again, casting their bodies into the sea, feeding and surviving.

If he could just have lasted a few more days, the old gull, I thought. But, I too was sucking in daylight, and I would not drown myself with the memory of the gull. I stepped on deck and inhaled deeply, feeding on real air, not that worn out stuff that still lingered in the cabin. I became stronger with just a few moments passing. I surveyed my body for storm damage. Yes, it could fish today. I ruffled my head and shoulders, gull-like, shaking residue sleep from me that was not needed.

Diesel engines were soon barking, as were the bull seals on the beach, and the harbor undulated once more with the wake of fishing boats. Gulls were overhead now.

I was confident, truly, and I based that on nothing more than the fact that I had had a good night's sleep. I did not wait for the weather report. I was hungry to devour the day. I was looking for handles by which to seize the day and show it my strength. I found them. The spokes of the helm of my boat.

The engine, remarkably, turned over the first time. The battery was alive, but it was shorting out somewhere along the line and I had to keep it charged by running the boat. Keeping the boat at an idle, as I had been forced to do for the week that I had been confined to the harbor, built up the carbon. I should have had the generator repaired, in fact, I might be able to pay for that soon.

This was the first day after a storm, and as it is with the gulls, so it is with the lobster fishermen. It is always easy after a storm and always a lot of money in it, but the ease diminishes into stability after a while, and it is the stability of the cycle to which we adjust ourselves, to which we proportion our ambition and plan our expenses. After a storm, the water settles and the lobsters can move freely again. When the water is agitated, they confine themselves to the caves and pot-holes, or head to deep water. When the water flattens out and things begin to settle, they are over loaded with hunger and are more easily seduced by the traps.

I was feeling like a fisherman that morning. I no longer had the walk of a man from the mainland, not that dry, lifeless gait. Mine was the step of a fisherman, and I knew it, smug as hell about it and I knew it. I secured the skiff to the mooring, and took my place at the wheel, and took the wheel in my hands and felt the day begin to flow, and my blood begin to flow, and I felt a part of it, the flow of the day and my blood. I was aware of the wonderful way in which my body adjusted itself to the pitch and the mild yaw of the boat and how effortlessly I was balanced, how I guided the wheel and did not lean on it.

I was feeling alive, released. We left the harbor like the subject of a painting leaves its canvas. We became animated. We were no longer defined by the frame of the harbor, or by its two dimensional waters.

I braced myself, not for the motion of the water I anticipated, but for what I might not see. I might not have seen an ocean calm enough to have permitted a day of fishing. I might have seen instead a surf torturing a shoreline, and if that were true I could not maneuver my boat near enough to fish my traps. As I thought these things, I felt my body stiffen against the wheel. I rounded Cat Head, and the perspective of the Island became more encompassing. For the first time in more than a week, I saw the Island, an island left out in a storm.

My eyes shot to the western tip of Catalina, where most of my traps laid. It was veiled, indistinct in a morning haze. The island is basically intact, but patches of fog, like sharks, had eaten away chunks of its flesh, making unfamiliar contours.

Sunlight can heal that, I thought. As it heals the gulls. As it heals me.

The sky was an indifferent gray, and the water beneath us muddy. The bow of the boat was pointed towards the first significant cove and we quartered the swells nicely. We were parting water well, parting water as a sloop parts water, and not like an old Monterey boat, parting water like Melissa parting her hair. The first cove, the first trial, upon us.

Time for a poker face. It might be empty. I saw the float for the first trap. It was straining against the high water of a storm tide. That's good, no slack line to get snagged in the prop.

I backed the boat around.

When we have a child, that's going to be our religion. I mean, everything is going to be sacrificed to him. That's why I can't do it yet. Don't want to share her with anyone else yet, even a child. A while longer, anyway. Pull the trap.

The boat was idling well, and Melissa took the wheel.

I slithered my way down the ladder from the bridge, and hooked the float. Melissa held the bow into the swells, giving just the right amount of throttle.

I threw the yellow propylene line over the winch, and stepped on the switch under its black diaphragm flush with the deck. The sound of the winch was like the sound of a portcullis in some old castle, rusty and grinding.

In clear water, I could look down as the traps approached the surface, and in the shallow water, I could sometimes even count what I had while it was still on the bottom. But this was storm weather, storm water, and I had no way of knowing until the traps broke the surface.

Probably, I will draw a blank, I told myself. Prepare yourself for that. Poker face intact? Good. Bad luck if the first one is full. Bad spot to drop a trap, too close to shore.

There was a mild thud, and I winced as if in pain, as if it were my own body and not the chine of the boat that had just been hit by the gouging corner of a rusted trap. I moved my foot over the disc on the deck to stop the winch.

In clear water fishing, I could slow the winch to prevent that sort of thing, I could see the traps coming and slowed them down. I consoled myself after a cursory look at the hull. Paint looked more like an accident than anything else, and flaked on the decks like psoriasis. It wasn't too bad on the deckhouse. Not quite respectable, but I could entertain myself with thoughts of hauling the boat and repainting it. The gouges that the trap had made would go unnoticed, and with a few days of weathering would look not unlike any of the other scars in the wood.

I looked over the rail, the corner of the cage now visible. I could see a trail of scars on the boat, as if from a flogging where traps had been dragged over the gun'lls onto the deck. Though the corner of the trap protruded from the muddied water, I could not see if the trap was full, and the corner looked distinctly like the head of an eel, staring at me, the rusted wire resembling the teeth. I stared once more at the place where the fangs had taken a bite of my boat, and reached into my back pocket for gloves.

I leaned over and put my hand in the mouth of the eel and started to pull. Melissa, from the vantage point of the helm, could see that there was no kelp wrapped around the trap as it balanced on the rail, so routinely then she edged the boat seaward. The Diesel murmured, but I shouted to be heard above it, "We're gonna eat tonight!" She turned her head down for a moment to see me holding two lobsters and she must have seen the others slapping their tales in the trap.

It was a good sign, I decided, for the first trap to be filled.

I quickly abandoned knowledge of my preconditioning for an empty trap and the things that that implied. When I finished sorting the ones that were legally large enough to keep from the others, I had four lobsters, and that was worth about twenty dollars, as they were exceptionally large.

I was grinning, as I changed places with my wife, and the caution that usually guided me was replaced with exuberance. It will be a good day. The traps are always full after a storm. I spun the old Monterey boat around, passed over the same spot, and when I made a fist, Melissa shoved the freshly baited trap over the stern.

A little blonde-haired boy. I blink, and he is beside me at the wheel. Women shout at me that to dream of having a boy is chauvinistic. *Dream of a child, but not a son,* they say. But I can't just dream of a cherub.

I looked for some land mark on the cliffs to help remember where we dropped the trap, to mark it on the chart. A goat stopped chewing on the grass just long enough to gaze in our direction, and then scamper further up the cliff.

Melissa could tell by my deliberate scanning that I was looking for a marker. She understood those things. "The cactus."

That would be a good landmark. I made a note on the chart. I dream of a little blond-haired boy, two years old, maybe three, pushing my legs apart while I'm at the wheel, like a little Sampson between two pillars, but then as we pitch with a swell, he wraps himself around me, around my leg. He's spinning and dancing and bare-footed and squirming, but he comes to me to sleep in my arms ... I must pull the traps now.

Melissa climbed up the ladder to join me.

"Hey, I was really nervous about the first trap, I mean, I'm just glad that it was full, something in it anyway," I said. "I should have laid more here. I think there's a reef running out about fifty yards." I indicated the lay of the reef with my hands. "Just hope it hasn't been sanded over by the storm currents."

I paused for a moment, plotting things out. "We'll save a few traps from the West End, drop them here on the way back." I checked out the fathometer. Yes, a reef, and in deep water away from the cliffs.

We were maneuvering towards a small promontory. I relinquished one arm from the helm and wrapped it around Melissa...a little round boy getting into everything.

Another buoy at the point. Melissa at the helm again, and I pulled the trap. Full. Another full trap. I unloaded it smiling and laughing. The day had just begun. I started to measure the lobsters. Three were keepers. That was not enough to get ecstatic about, but it was only the second trap. I showed as much reserve and calm as I could, but it was hard, knowing that it was only the second trap and I had almost sixty more to go.

I could see the gulls already on the kelp. I was happy for them. The sun, the shadow-maker for them, was assuming his throne.

I took the wheel again. When I have a son, when I have my baby boy, he will not sleep alone. He will be cradled between Melissa and me, when he sleeps, when we sleep. I shall not abandon him when he's born, or ever. We won't be an island to him—we'll be a harbor ... . Another trap, around the point, I think.

I looked ahead, to where the buoy should have been.

There was only muddied water. Ok. That's only one trap. Not deep enough, or not enough scope. The storm tide and swells had wrenched it free, the buoy from the line. Or maybe it had been carried into deeper water and the float was straining for the surface. That was possible. I would have to wait for the water to clear, at least a few days. I might find it then, and pull it with a grappling hook. I will just have to wait. It would have been better to have remained straight-faced, indifferent. It seems to be the way to handle disappointment.

I looked at Catalina once. Perhaps I had made a mistake. No, it was the right cove. The sun was just on the cliffs now, throwing color on the surf. I could hear the surf on the promontory. I was tired. I was still close to sleep, as close as the early hour was to the night that had passed. Only that I am tired, I reasoned, but the surf sounds distinctly like fire. When I am more awake, it will be surf again, but now it is fire. I wiped my brow.

I found another trap and pulled it. Two lobsters, I think. I baited it. I was somehow detached. The sound of the surf again. Then I realized that there should have been more traps in that cove. I double checked the markings on my chart. Three traps. Three traps missing. I thought the cove was better protected. Another ten yards seaward would have put them deeper. Catalina drops off that quickly. Another ten yards. I looked at what I had in the hold. Not enough to pay for three traps. Maybe enough for two. If they are not broken up on the bottom, I might find them when the water clears. I looked back on the deck, remembering the traps I had sold. Skeletal though they were, they had protected the gull. Protection. I wish now I had not sold them … . When we have a son, he will sleep between us. We will be his wings. We shall flank him. We shall spread ourselves for him, and fold ourselves all around him, when he wants it … .

The other traps had better be full. I brought the boat around, the old Monterey with the rolled bottom and soft chine. Not flat, like a coastal lobster boat. It could be forgiving in a sea, but it rolled like a son-of-a-gun, and as I spun the wheel to port, and put the throttle to the Gray Marine engine, we were metted by our own wake, and staggered and rolled out of the cove.

Another familiar land point. I envisioned my traps on the other side. I made a very clear picture in my mind of what the floats would look like, bobbing there. I rounded the point.

Nothing.

Melissa looked at me, testing her fear upon my face. I could feel my jaw tighten.

The boat was moving forward again. I did not scan for long the vacant cove. We were not moving with enough power to steer the boat well. Reluctantly, I moved the throttle forward a notch. I took the wheel in both hands. I swear the surf sounds like fire.

"There's one," Melissa pointing, and I was on it. I backed the boat around, positioned it, bypassed more rungs on the ladder than I should have, and I was on it. I snagged it with the boat hook, wrapped the yellow line on the winch and pulled. This time, no hesitation for the sake of the hull.

The abuses made by the trap would be just one more scar, nothing fatal. Just haul the trap.

It came tumbling down over the rail. *"Gloves!"* I'd forgotten. I looked at my hands. Little rivers of red water on my palms. I don't like manhandling the traps, but this one came tumbling down on the deck, breaking off the legs of the lobsters that dangled through the wire cage. I opened the rusted door, and started to reach for the lobsters. I was on one knee, and before I touched the first one, I realized that it was insane, being so delicate, and I stood up, took the bottom of the trap, and flipped it over on the deck.

The lobsters, six or eight of them, were scrambling to right themselves, as they slapped themselves on the deck, each lost in a maze that had no walls. I took the largest and held it up to the gage to see if it was big enough to sell.

"HEY!" A scream from the helm.

I was moving too fast and I should have brought the boat further from the shore. I had the panic-anger, and like a rock is thrown into the wheels of an advancing tank, I threw the lobster into the foaming, rapid-like foaming, muddy surf.

That close, in the surf zone. We're in the surf.

I mounted the station. I jammed the throttle full forward and the thrust almost took me down, but I was buried into the wheel, one hand holding on to one of its stout wooden spokes. The other arm reaches for the yellow headed boy but he has vanished. One swell, a remnant storm swell, was passing under the bow, heaving under the boat, and the swell even broke into white water under the stern.

And then the whole boat just dropped; a pocket of the ocean had opened up and we fell into it. We hit hard. For a moment the prop churned only the air and screamed, unmuffled. The ribs of the boat, the planks of the boat, somehow held together, but Christ, they must have hurt.

Water spattered us, even on the bridge, and I heard things crashing together, breaking, dishes, below. We went out another thirty yards, into the deep water, and the sea was flat and innocent again.

Standing by my shoulder, holding onto the combing of the wind-screen, Melissa, heaving, fighting for air.

"Too short," I said, "Take the wheel."

I was on the deck again, and scooped up the squirming lobsters and tossed them over the rail. I reached into the bait tin, and yanked out a bewildered fish heads and baited the rusting, twisted trap. I set it on the fantail. Blood on my hands from I don't know where. It doesn't seem to matter. No, it doesn't matter, just one more abuse. Pull the traps. I coiled line beside the trap and swapped places with Melissa. I circled once around. My fingers knotted above me. Give me your tired, your poor. Melissa dumped the trap into the hungry muddiness as my hand came down.

She came back to the helm. "All short," I said, "all of them."

I did not look at her now. Pull the traps. My gaze became gyro-scopic, fixed on the next spit of land, and if the bow deviated from the point, my hands, both of them firmly on the wheel now, corrected it.

Still flat. The water is still flat, but it must be past nine o'clock. Another two hours, and it will begin. The wind. Gentle first, probing first. But I will not be deceived. I've got three hours maybe. Now, while my hair is not blown into disarray, and my brow does not buckle to keep the wind off my eyes.

I reached a nameless point, and spun the wheel once more, and pulled the throttle back. Blood caked to my hand. It must have been from the fish head. I don't remember feeling cut, but my hands were a bit numb anyway, and would not have felt it. There is occasional mercy, at least, in fishing. I scanned the small inlet.

Nothing.

"I had two traps here." Too shallow. I dropped them too shallow. Maybe I can come back here, too, with a grappling hook. It's hard with a big boat.

I held the throttle again, a chess-piece, in three fingers. I delib-erated over my next move. I edged the throttle forward, keeping my hand on the knob, leaving the option open for a different tactic. No. Leave this cove. It's dry. Its dry like … Melissa, from the corner of my eye, kept the thought from completing itself. I deserve to see the traps, I mean, I worked for it. Isn't that the bargain we all make with God?

There was no fuel gauge to watch, to make me anxious, but I knew that the throttle full forward meant that the Diesel was gorging on fuel. The smoke frightened me. It needs oil, new oil, and if I don't get new oil, it will need new rings.

And if I don't get new rings, it will need a new engine. That's how it happened before. It can happen again. Paint? Shit. That can wait. So can the caulking. Anyway, it has stopped storming now, and I don't need to caulk the cabin top. I tell myself, if you caulk it now, you might seal in some of the rainwater, and it's the rainwater that carries the little spores that cause dry rot. Let it air out. Wait a week, a month, but do not degrade your intelligence by buying caulking while that bastard of an engine needs oil!

As I rounded an anonymous point, the first hint of wind scratched its way across my forehead, not to test my strength yet, just to taunt me a bit. I rolled my watch cap down, visor-like, and Melissa came from below with a sandwich. Then a gust of wind that I did not anticipate sandpapered its way over the bow of the boat. Too early in the day to have to contend with that, too. Though it was only a gust, it was a reminder that it could be worse, and a reminder that the wind and water had no respect for my frail concepts of morality, that it would blow in spite of the bargain I thought I had with God. It's not fair; it is not fair. My muscles began flexing with the wind, and as the day intensified itself, so would I. I do not, I cannot, attack. That much I had learned. I save my strength to parry the blows.

SIX

Ribbon Rock.

The most protected cove.

I could see the blueness of the water from a distance.

A deep bottom and hard granite cliffs that do not easily erode to muddy the water. It existed like a small eddy, a grotto, generally left intact when it stormed. But still, I could not see into the cove. I had no way of knowing. I had only the microscopic history of the morning upon which to make predictions. But what should I believe? That protected coves will save me? I was losing. I had no reason to believe that the traps would be spared. I leaned forward at the wheel, as if by so doing, I would be there that much sooner.

They must be there. Please, be there. The history of the day saying *no*. There are six traps there, I put them there. They should be there!

I was chewing the bread, the sandwich she had made. There was meat in the sandwich, but I was only aware that I was chewing the bread.

I pulled nearer to the cove.

Six floats.

I had come from desert to oasis. All six floats. Good.

I can forget the rational I had prepared for myself if there had been five. The lies I would tell myself if there were four. The anxiety, if there were three. The desperation, if there were two, only two, the frustration, if there was only one, the defeat, if it was another empty cove, the philosophy to console me.

All six.

I dropped the throttle back. Slow down. They are yours. Just slow down and one after another. This cove could do it. If there are two dozen, you can break even today, replacing the lost traps with used ones.

New ones are out of the question, unless, of course, there are three dozen, instead of two. It could happen. All six traps, protected. And probably in this cove, protected as it is, the lobsters have been feeding normally, and I haven't been here in six or seven days, to pull.

Maybe even more than three dozen.

But have I learned nothing today? Do not trap yourself with optimism. They are empty, every one. Tell yourself that. If you can deceive yourself into thinking that they are full, then you can convince yourself that they are empty. Tell yourself that lie, and then there is the astonishment when they are full. It doesn't matter. In a half an hour the feelings can order themselves properly, according to a need, according to what is or what isn't. Just pull the traps. These little philosophies are the things to entertain you when your tired body is finished with all this, when all this is over this evening on the way home. Now just pull the traps.

I could do it all so much faster with a small boat, not this polar bear. But now, I have the big boat, and subsequently, many small pauses, into which little dreams and ambitions fill, like rainwater on a high cliff fills in little cracks. My empty time, little crevasses. And when the traps are empty, the water will freeze. I will feel my back stiffen a little with every empty trap. Like water freezing, and then little chips of granite are displaced by ice. And the granite falls. Work hard. Do not allow water into the little cracks on the high cliffs. Do not allow dreams to fill the empty time. Pull the traps. That's always worked. Pull the empty traps.

Sustain your indifference, I told myself. My head could do that, but my body was betraying me. I was moving too fast, hungry to taste just one triumphant day. Nothing to get excited about. A triumph is only a mild accomplishment that does not encounter resistance. Like going the whole day without stubbing your toe.

Or cutting your hand.

It was not the blood from a fish head. I moved my fingers. A mild sting. Not enough to weave a martyrdom out of, not enough to bring Melissa around, but still annoying. I sucked my fingers as I wrapped the yellow line of the first trap around the winch. It then became a mechanical thing, the trap coming to the surface of the water in the basin of the high cliff. That protected cove.

Water was clearer here. I could see the outline of the trap about twenty feet below the surface. My eyes must be lying to me, or making credible other lies that I have told myself. I could not make out the forms, but the traps were dark, full, bulging with lobsters! I said nothing. The line was straining. Heavy with lobsters. I said nothing. A paddy of kelp hovered over the trap, making its features indistinct, but there was no doubt that it was full.

The trap surfaced, and I stopped the winch. Kelp on top of the trap. Slow down. Don't let things get out of hand. That was good, stopping the winch. Try to pull the trap out of the water with that much kelp on it and the line might snap.

I could not take my eyes off it. The kelp was thick. I leaned over the rail, and called for the knife.

The *knife* was a pock-marked machete that cleared kelp from the anchor often enough, and decimated the albacore I wired into the traps for bait. There was too much salt water and salt air to worry about keeping it sharp, but it could hack off the kelp. She handed me the knife, and I didn't tell her it was full, as she walked back to the helm. I wanted her to see it on deck. I wanted her to see my casual indifference to it.

Do it slowly, I said to myself. The kelp, a web over the traps, the last obstacle. The wind, the rain, these were things that at best, I could only adapt to, but the kelp was something I could attack. Do it slowly, I said to myself. My disobedient body, with more force than was necessary, brought the blade down and I started to chop. Once. Twice. It started to come, but the third blow, a mild rolling of the boat, the blow misplaced, and it sliced through the taught thin yellow line and the trap was lost. The knife was on the deck, and my hand was over my cheek, the line having snapped me in the face before the frayed end unraveled on the deck. I leaned over the rail to see the cubicle drift downward, sinking out of my sight into eighty feet of water.

I was coiling yellow line in one hand.

Melissa had taken the boat slowly from the cliff, giving me a moment more to recover. She had, of course, seen it all from the helm, but she could not have seen inside the trap. I stood, having been seated on the fish-hold, and I looked at my hand, after feeling my cheek. No blood. No fresh blood, anyway. But the line had stung, and I felt as if it had cut me.

I came up to the helm, and looked at Melissa, though not into the gavel of her eyes.

"It was empty," I said, and I took the helm. "No, that's not right. It was full, at least ten or twelve in it." I looked at her sadly. Tears from the sting, but she could think that they were for her, if she liked. Her face showed me nothing. Then she looked at my cheek, and saw that it was red and was swelling. She kissed it once, but with an unchanging face, and stepped below, leaving me alone to punish myself for my lie and for my incompetence.

But the punishment was not self-inflicted. The wind had a way to dig at me now, to make its judgment of me known. I had been covered, protected from exposure, but my cheek was raw now, and the wind delighted in that discovery, as the rain had delighted in finding a small hole in the top of the cabin during the last few evenings.

Melissa stayed below, and I will never know what she did. I pulled the next five traps from the protected cove without incident.

They were empty.

—ww— SEVEN —ww—

The sound of the Diesel, the drone, numbed me. I was grateful
for that. I had felt enough, too much, and there was nothing else that
I wanted to feel. The drone was a wall all around me. But I was to dis-
cover that it was not impenetrable. There was only the West End now,
only the West End held out any hope for salvaging what was left of the
day. The wind feigned no gentleness. It came from the ocean, not the
gentle land breeze. It came like locust.

As the probability of mild success diminished, I charged forth
from still another empty cove. The West End was arching before me, a
half an hour away. I had only a small number of traps between Ribbon
Rock and the West End, so at first I deviated from the island's perimeter, and thought of cutting right across the arch and going straight
into the West End. I broke away from the island like a bull must break
away from its chute and is attacked first by the immensity of the arena.
The throttle was full forward. I had to chance it. It made the boat
vibrate, more than move forward, and it snorted black Diesel from its
nostrils and stumbled over the small waves, and trenched through the
thick swells, and its hooves powdered the air with spume as if it were
dust and sand, and deep within its chest pulsated a Diesel engine that
breathed and bellowed and grunted.

It was a bull and it was awesome, but only as a bull in an arena
is awesome, only seen out of context was it powerful. A bull is energy
seduced by a red cloak and ultimately a bull is not led into an arena to

kill a matador, but to be killed. Why must I think like this? Why can I not just think about how good it will be to get back to the harbor and secure and drink a cup of coffee? Yes, we have plenty now, a large can. The wind is picking up, directly from the West End, now. The swells are picking up. The surf, too.

It would be good to drink a cup of coffee now. You have only to turn this wheel once, hold for a moment, and then straighten it again. Melissa will understand. You have enough to eat for the next few days anyway. Melissa will understand that too. It's been too frustrating today, to risk another defeat. The traps at the West End might be lost, or empty. And if they are, what is there tonight? What then, if they are empty, could possibly pull me out of the harbor tomorrow? I know that the traps in the West End are in deep water, all of them. And in a storm, the lobsters would also have to go deep. And there is also the full moon. That means higher and lower tides. And the lower tides mean the lobsters are going to be milked out of the shallows, and they have to go deep. Pull the traps.

I pulled away from the island, not caring for the few traps that I might or might not have found along the perimeter. It was two o'clock. The wind was anything but discrete now, as I headed for the West End. I was determined to pull the traps. Melissa, can you see that? Can you see that even though the wind is picking up a few hours early, I am heading for the West End?

The boat rolled with every irregularity of the sea, and whitecaps, just unavoidably, were making themselves visible, at first as only a few spontaneous bursts, but then with greater frequency and density. I had been going fifteen minutes towards the West from the point at which I had disembarked with my decision to pull the traps that waited there. But I still had half an hour to go. The wind had picked up and slowed us down. In fifteen minutes, would it still be a half an hour? I started counting. Two. Three. Storm ratings. Count the densities of the little whitecaps and relate them to some insane numerical chart that tells you if it is storming. The whitecaps, bursting like popcorn, now. Melissa, a half an hour ago I made the decision to pull the traps at the West End. To expose myself to one more defeat. Did you know that? Did you see that? Did you?

But I am thinking of coffee now. I am seducing myself.

I am thinking that I have only to turn this wheel for a moment, and straighten it, and then each moment brings us closer to the harbor, instead of away from it. I am thinking also how sweet is the taste of my own sleep. And her body, too. I really do want to pull the traps.

Spume was insulting me, at the wheel. Spitting at me as I came down off each wave. Melissa, let me go back to the harbor. When I turn this wheel, and you come from below, to see what I am doing, look at my swollen cheek. Look at the salt water dousing me, and understand. And the wind. It's pulling me from the wheel. It's strong. I can hold on. I can pull the traps, but it's so hard with the wind and all. It would be easier with a smaller boat. I've got more area exposed to the wind than a sailboat.

I am so willing to do it, but the sea is so uncooperative. Tell me you are sea sick, tell me you are tired, tell me that you wish that we were in the harbor drinking coffee, having a warm meal. Tell me these things Melissa, help me turn this wheel around.

I felt cold, with the wind.

I heard the hatch open, but the engine drowned the more subtle sounds of the woman's footsteps. She came to my side. She took the combing to balance herself. The wind was trying to steal the hair from her forehead.

"Want my cap?"

"No," her eyes blinking in the wind.

"You don't have to stand up here."

"I don't mind."

Melissa, why do you say that? Why can't you say this is torture? Why can you not see that it is? Why don't you ask me to turn this thing around? Melissa, I'll be truthful with you. I don't mind the wind and the cold, not that much. But if we get to the West End, and there is nothing, what then? Then the harbor will be more than two hours away. Then I will have to hang onto this goddamn wheel and it will be cold when we get to the harbor. There will be no way to get through the night if the West End is empty. I don't even mind my cheek. A few days and I'll have forgotten it. Melissa, I want to be honest with you, let me be honest with you. But help me to be honest with you. Make the first move. Tell me it's torturous up here. It really is. Tell me that we should turn around and do it in the morning. First thing, the West End.

Melissa was silent.

She was smiling. I was fastened to the wheel by her smile. Pull the traps, I said. Pull the traps, pull the traps, pull the traps.

"Melissa?"

"   ." Nothing, but her attention.

"That wind is really picking up. We could pull the traps, but it would be hell in this wind. I think we ought to hit it first thing in the morning. The West End. Bypass all the other traps which we can pull on the way in. What do you think?"

"It's up to you." She meant it.

Why could she not have made it easier? Why could she not say, "I think you are right?" Why this faith in me? Why? Oh shit.

I said nothing. I made a very large arc. As we paralleled the swells, the boat took its most dramatic healing.

The West End was lurched out of the horizon. Then there was the open sea, and then, as the boat came around, in the distance was Cat Head, the harbor.

There was something that resembled relief, with the wind driving us home. On my shoulders, now, instead of in my face.

My eyes fixed on the harbor. The salt spray, no more, not then as we were going with the wind instead of into it. My cheek felt better.

Sun on the cliffs now, but still light I think, when we reach the harbor. The deep blue is coming from the bottom, replacing the muddied water that was here this morning. Hope this is the last of it, this wind.

But eventually I saw the act for what it was: retreat.

The wind was filling my sweater, my amber sweater. It was strong, but I stayed secured to the wheel, and I clung to the wheel like the flame to a wick of a candle. The wind screamed by, and I was not extinguished.

The harbor was the vanishing point of the horizon of my thoughts. I was not traveling as one integrated body, on my way to the harbor. My warmth was pulled from me, and waited for me there. My eyes, of course, saw nothing but me, there, in the harbor secured to the mooring, emptying my head of the sound of the Diesel, and my nostrils of its smell. My muscles had abandoned me. They waited in the harbor, too, in the harbor where I could once again be intact and at peace. My hair, blowing to the harbor like a telltale, pointing the way.

I closed my eyes.

My body stood on the stern deck of my boat, waiting for me to return from a long day of fishing. My mouth was dry.

I swallowed. Dryness all down my throat. I turned and looked over my shoulder. A following sea, and the West End looked heavy with swells. That was a comfort. It could have flattened out. It could have mocked me. It was rough. Heading home now had justification. Too rough. I could rest.

The sun was over the West End, and the water shimmered like flame. The sun was raining fire on the water. But soon I will be in the harbor.

It will happen eventually. I might as well let it happen now. Time to tabulate the score. The harbor will be there, whether you do or don't.

Eight lobsters, as opposed to eight dozen. But I have never done eight dozen in a day. That's thirty dollars, maybe. Maybe a little less. I shouldn't have broken the legs off. I think that will cost me. The water drains from them that way. Paid by the pound. Enough for fuel and little else. But I must be precise, how much else?

My thoughts circled over me like gulls, waiting for me to toss scraps.

I should have gotten the smaller sized coffee.

But there is thirty dollars. Depend on that. Create a strategy based on that. It is an entirely different strategy than one based on twenty dollars, or ten. Or three hundred.

Well, I think I've done it all, gone through it all. No disappointments ahead. Only if the boat stops.

No, I think not.

It's too narcissistic, the Diesel. Loves its own sound, its own power. I can really slow down now, allow myself to feel. Let the Diesel chant me into the harbor. It's over for today. Thank god.

I was having trouble keeping the bow pointed to Cat Head. It kept straying a bit. Must be the swells, I thought. We kept faltering, drifting left or right.

My hands on the wheel were most forgiving. It's over for the day. The swells seemed to correct the course, holding the boat to the harbor. Almost as if all this water drained away through the harbor, pulling everything through it. The gulls were returning. The wind brought it to an end for them, too. The other fishermen, of course. Faster boats.

The decks were dripping with kelp. I smelled it for the first time, just then. Not an unpleasant smell, at all. Fresh. Salt air, too. That was good. And sunset dripping with color.

Moist. These things, I suppose, attracted us to fishing. I was feeling it now, dead tired. But it was over for the day, over. In fact, don't even plan tomorrow yet. I know I will have to hit the West End first, and hit it early. I'll take it from there. It could have been worse today. Eight lobsters, thirty dollars. The harbor getting closer. Pass Cat Head and it's finished for today. Just a little while longer, and nothing else can hurt me for today, really. At least, I don't have to tell Melissa about my failure, she had seen it all, been part of it. No explanations to make, nothing to detract from the comfort of the harbor, and it comes closer with each swell. Blankets probably are dry now, too. Good to blow out the candle and feel the weight of the blankets over me.

I looked over my shoulder, down on the decks. Melissa. More a silhouette than Melissa, the sun in my eyes. Pretty, though. I hope she understands why it will be so artless tonight. Do you know, Melissa, how afraid I am of that now? You will think it's a vent. You will think I do to you what I could not do to the day—win. It's not like that really, win or lose with you. It's just that I've been robbed of any ability to be delicate today, by all that's happened, and I've had to be so harsh. I don't want to say no to it, the release you need as much as I do. You will know then how defeated I am. But I don't really want it, knowing how it's going to be. Strong and swift and a door to sleep. I don't want that. But you can help me. Fall asleep before I come to you, fall asleep when I check the mooring.

She turned from watching the sea behind us and examined the day's catch.

Pitiful, isn't it? Eight, or was it seven? I have forgotten, but it's about thirty dollars. We will keep then in the floating receiver when we leave in the morning. Probably I will tell you these things when we moor. Something for the time between eating and sleeping. The harbor getting closer, almost through.

She picked up the largest one, the one from the first trap.

I could see it. Worth maybe six dollars. Two days groceries. A half a dozen eggs times ten. The harbor was getting closer. Melissa, do you know how happy it makes me to see your hair blowing like that?

She turned the lobster over on its back.

She shot the words at me! "It's a female!"

My weight dropped like a gallows door, and I pulled the throttle back. I came down from the tower. She was right, a bright orange cluster of eggs under the tail, a female and as such, not legal to sell. I looked at Melissa in disbelief.

How could she make such a discovery? Something strange to me came from within me and my hand twisted at the end of my arm like a moray eel.

"NO, IT'S NOT!" words speaking, imprisoned in my tightened jaw. I ripped the roe from the tale, and threw it over the side, and I dropped the lobster back in the hold.

She was astonished and ashamed and so was I, and I went back to the wheel, where she did not join me.

Ah, Melissa, the harbor was so close.

So close.

Sails on the horizon, white and jagged, a regatta of sharks' teeth, devour what is left of the day.

—ᴡᴡ— EIGHT —ᴡᴡ—

Experience taught me the morning sounds of Catalina, so the mystery in them was gone. I knew them all. The gulls screaming was usually first, followed by the goats bleating on the hill. Then the slapping on the hull would intensify, and as the wind shifted or the tide changed, the water and oil and blood in the bilge would slosh like a mop in a wash bucket.

Planks which I had never identified and could only approximate would begin flexing, working, mild strains that didn't threaten us. But I could hear them. Each plank had a distinct pitch, being of different densities and lengths, like strings in a piano. There was also the contracting of the mooring line through the chock, the friction that always was unnerving, but which had been proven to be harmless by experience, the mooring always intact when I checked it. There was the little sucking sound of the kelp on the mooring line, plunging and rising off the water as the hemp became taught and then slack, and taught again.

Somehow these sounds, though never in particular order, never seemed to overlap themselves, were always synchronized. I knew all the sounds and was intimate with them. They ushered me from my sleep.

There was something then, (something) that exploded like mutiny, when I pulled my hand from Melissa, pulled open the small curtain and the rays of the sun slanted through the windows and over the small table with the absolute certainty of at least eleven o'clock!

I had heard nothing and it was eleven o'clock!

My god! To have slept through it!

I lunged from the bunk, ripping the blanket from Melissa as I did, and it trailed off the bunk onto the floor. I slid open the hatch, like rolling away the stone.

I stumbled as I stepped out into the sunlight, the pure golden sunlight, and saw a day half way down the tracks.

Quickly, I mounted the bridge to look out to the harbor mouth, almost hoping that it was swollen shut with swells. It laid open before me, flat. Absolutely flat.

The harbor was deserted. No gulls, no fishing boats. I slept through even their primeval cries. The goats were on the hill picking at the grass, unhurried. No one in the harbor, no one in the trough of the isthmus even to see me in my nakedness, or my humiliation. I pumped the starter switch, not surveying the gauges as I descended into the cabin and my blue jeans, Melissa sitting up in bed in bewilderment.

"It's NOON! I said.

"Oh my god!"

"And it's flat. I mean it's perfect!"

Bare-footed. No time for a shirt. I pulled my watch-cap off the table, and it was on my head as I charged through the hatch again. I pulled the skiff to the bow and made it fast to the mooring line. My god, I only hope the engine is warmed up, I thought, knowing that it wasn't. It can stall and if it stalls we're had. We are had because I'm casting us free, right now!

I tossed the slimed mooring line off the bitt, and I scaled the cabin and took the helm. Oh fuck! Not a boat in the harbor.

And it's perfect.

The throttle did not have the enjoyment of easing in so slowly. It didn't matter if I made a wake anyway. No boats in the harbor to be rocked or to complain about it. Not good though, for the Diesel. Fuck the Diesel.

There was a shirt on my shoulders before I reached the harbor mouth. Thank you, Melissa. She too was bare-footed, but she came up to the pinnacle with my boots, and she took the wheel without speaking. I wrestled my socks and boots over wet feet, trapping in the salt water, the decks upon which I had been walking never really drying, not even in the sun, the goddamn noonday sun that was on us. Nothing was said, as was becoming typical of all our conversations. This was a very serious blunder, waking so late, and it left an imperative: The West End. That transcended conversation.

The wind was prowling from the west down to the east as we left the shelter of Cat Head. My feet shuffled as I guided the wheel, my weight shifted from one leg to the other. Energy was rolling in my shoulders, falling down inside an arm to my hand, and there it stiffened, and trudged up my shoulders again, and down the other arm. The energy, pacing, looking for a flaw in my body, some way to escape, pacing, looking. Tensing.

Pull the traps. The traps will be something upon which I can unleash all this. This I said to the energy that was stalking through the foliage of my body, through the muscles of my body. But there was no peace in that, in the words. I stiffened.

My eyes allowed nothing, nothing but the West End. I wanted to look at the gauges. I had started the boat too fast, no time for a warm-up. That can be disastrous to its cycle. The temperature, both oil and water must be just right. Other little things too that I did not want to imagine. But I did not look at the panel. I knew that if I looked, something might be out of order. And if it is out of order, the West End will become more distant. Don't look at the gauges. Think of the traps. Think of pulling the traps.

Minutes strained themselves by.

Somewhere from below came Melissa, with a cup of hot coffee in her hands. For that, I will allow a distraction. But not the eyes. They keep to the West End. Not even a glance of thanks. But I am certain, why, as certain as I am that I love the woman that she understood I must look only at the West End. I became dedicated to that.

Gulls overhead, competing for my attention, lost, to the West End. I raised the coffee and sipped. I could hear the whining engines of the other lobster boats from time to time, bouncing off of cliffs into the open water. But I would even glance in their direction, as I barreled forward, and if I looked at the instrument panel, when I looked back up the West End will have vanished. I took a chance and checked the oil temperature, then the pressure. The West End again. Then the water pressure. The West End. Temperature. West End. Fix it in your eyes for a moment, and in your hands. That's it. Now the rpms.

Good. All was in order. The engine even sounded good. I allowed myself the luxury of thinking that, and as the minutes passed, and no irregularities were detected, I allowed myself to accept it as fact. Yes. The engine is running well. The West End.

Half the day is melted away. I slept through it. God that made me tired. Like forgetting to blow out the candle when I fell asleep. Just wasted. I will have to hurry now. No time for the little thoughts that keep me alive. There are only the traps. All that exists are the traps, yet, a half remembrance was still vexing me. My thoughts were pulling themselves together, like newly braided mooring line pulls itself together under stress, straightening itself out and strengthening.

Gradually, though I wished only to think about the traps, the thought of the first wakeful moment, the thought that I so abruptly pulled myself from this morning, broke my obsession with the traps and the West End. Pull the traps…later.

Now, I want to think, indeed, I can only think, of early this morning. No wait a minute. That was not early this morning. It was the few moments before I was truly awake, but it was certainly not early. No way can I say that. It was before I pulled away from her. Yes. I remember now. I think Melissa knows. We have not spoken about it, but she sees my eyes floating down between her breasts and her hips. She takes my hand now, and holds it to her, where my eyes have been, when she sees that I've been watching, holds my hand to her and wraps herself around it like it's all right, and I feel her body move. I think before my hands used to settle on her breast, or in the gentle valley just under her neck. Yes, that's the way it was but not lately. That is where I used to find my hand in the morning when I woke up, and sometimes she'd be holding it to her there. But, lately, as I think of it, my hand has been over her womb when I wake up. I think she must know. Before I pulled open the curtain this morning. My hand.

It was still warm. Oh, she must know.

Damn, that I can't think these things now. The West End. I abandoned the thought of my child not yet conceived. Cut the thought loose and let it drift. And it drifted slowly from me, like a sailboat drifts from the mainland, until it is no longer distinguishable among other thoughts. There is now only one acceptable thought. The others, in time, but not now.

The West End, in the distance, and as I drifted from the thought of Melissa and the child, I seemed to drift closer to the West End.

I could see a patch of kelp, one of the many freed by the storm, drifting ahead of us. Its loose fronds dangled and curled, and experience told me it was something to avoid. I don't think I could handle having the propeller getting wrapped up in kelp. On another day, perhaps, but today has only room for the West End, the traps there, and little else. Nothing else.

I turned the wheel forty-five degrees to avoid the kelp. Gulls that had been perched there, feeding and resting and sunning as I knew they would, seemed to know that my evasive maneuver was not a courtesy to them, but for my own survival. So no show of gratitude on their part, or even a glance in my direction.

The bow was now pointing to a new stretch of island. It was that easy. The West End was no longer the center of my course or of my attentions. Be reasonable, that's within me. I have twelve traps between here and the West End that I didn't get to yesterday. Pull those first.

If the wind picks up heavily by two as it did yesterday, I won't be able to hold the boat in place. I'll be pulled off. It's just too big, too much sail area. I could already see the small boats, the lobster skiffs, headed home.

I decided to keep to the first available traps, the mild fanaticism about the West End having served its function, having gotten me out of the harbor and established the imperative before me—to pull some traps and get some fucking money.

Melissa, I wish you would come up here, so that I could just pull you to me. Maybe lean against the combing to keep from falling.

Pull you to me. Like pulling a trap? With that kind of desperation, like maybe it will be all tangled, or even empty? Pulling the mooring line over the bitt to secure. Pulling away from an anchorage or a harbor, or from Melissa ... Pulling my way through another day, or a night. Pulling myself from the bunk. Pulling my hand from her, and the blanket. Pulling myself together. Pulling myself through one more season. Jesus, is there just nothing that flows?

And now, I must pull, pull a trap. I saw one and began maneuvering.

The stern carved its way towards the island as I pulled ...

... NO! Not *pulled:* The stern of my boat carved its way towards the island as I *turned* the wheel to port. I throttled into reverse, backing away from the direction of the West End, which stared at us belligerently. Melissa had just come up. Tomorrow, maybe even later today, the West End, but now, I must ...

... A quick whine that meant a drop in rpms!

I threw the gear into neutral to keep the prop from turning. Bits of orange Styrofoam in the wake of the stern. Melissa just buried her head in her arm, her face starving for the right expression, but hiding her poverty in her arm.

First trap, first float. I'd run over it.

Killed it like a dog in the street.

Broke it. Lost it.

I swear the surf sounds like fire.

I threw the gears in forward again, as I was drifting still with inertia towards a wash-rock. Line in the prop, making us powerless.

Full bore, open.

We surged forward, strands of yellow propylene emerging behind us, frayed and floating. Nothing for me to do. I pulled …damn that word… I pulled the throttle back again, and for a moment, with the safety from a little forward motion, I jumped to the deck and ran to the stern. I grasped the rail and looked into the water, to see if I was trailing any line, to see if the water was clear enough to see the trap.

Muddy. Shallow water, but muddy.

I returned to the bridge, heavy as I ascended with the weight of Melissa's eyes upon me. There was just nothing to say. I knew that for a long time there would be nothing to say. The first trap. The first trap.

Her face was listless, like a full sail in a dead wind.

I was afraid that maybe I had pulled it into deep water. That was possible. As I pulled forward, I might have pulled it off the ledge, if I hadn't severed the line by then. It drops fast here. I could tell by the way the surf broke but I gauged that against the fathometer. Yes. Sixty feet or better here. If I pulled it off, I'll never find it. Nothing to do but wait until the water clears. If I didn't jerk it into deep water, I can find it.

Water, lapping against the boat like the surging within a heart, my heart lapping inside me like the water against the hull. The rays of the sun bent my brow over my anvil eyes. The water was still dulled, but the granite had been polished by the recent rains, and the cliff mirrored and intensified the light, making the next float almost indistinct upon the water. As if the trap were a living thing, as if it were something that could be frightened away, I made my approach. I acted delicately, or so I commanded my hands on the wheel. I could not allow myself to lose another trap.

Melissa took the helm, and I took the gaff.

I snared the float and pulled it to me, and the line, mossy now for being so long unattended, was soon twining on the winch. I depressed the power button on the deck and the line was coiling itself.

The trap, with what I at one time thought of as being routinely, broke the surface, and I hauled it onto the deck. I opened the rusting gate, and pulled two seemingly live and healthy lobsters from the skeletal remains of two or three others. It was quite clear. It was as I had thought, the dead lobsters acting as fresh bait for the others. Cannibals.

I put fresh fish trimmings in the canister, but I left the carcasses enmeshed in the wire, anticipating that their scent could still draw fish. I examined the lobsters that I now had in the hold, and I satisfied myself that they were healthy enough. With nothing that resembled enthusiasm, I nodded my head and Melissa edged the boat seaward. I launched the trap myself this time.

How could I have slept so long? A condemnation more than a question.

As I stood on the bridge, I realized that I should have inspected the yellow line. It may have been rotting or aging under the moss. It's not very expensive and I would hate to lose a trap to something like that. One or two good days of fishing, and I can replace the line.

The moss had a very unhealthy feel on my hands. Oh yes, the gloves. Don't forget the gloves for the next trap. Melissa worked her way from the bridge, and started down the ladder. "They're *males*," I said. That halted her, and for a few indecisive moments, she clung to the ladder, but was then beside me again. I could see the next trap. It seemed to be where I had left it. It was a good sign. This part of the island seems to be more protected than the other stretches. The traps were not migrating with the storm water. Next winter I will know, and when the storm season comes, I will fish heavy here, in this little half-moon.

The boat pivoted, and sent little folds of water toward the float. It bobbed as if at one moment it would sink, or as if it might pop free from the line. It did neither. With caution, and with gloves, I hauled the second trap over the rail and onto the over-worked decks. I could see sailboats rounding the West End in the distance.

That was good. At this hour of the day if can only mean that they are coming into Cat Harbor for the night. I can sell them what is in the fish hold. There is not that much. It can save me a day running into Avalon. I can unload what I caught yesterday.

Two more lobsters, not abundantly healthy. I tossed them into their cell. When the Monterey boat was built, it was with a bait tank that circulated water and held live sardines to fish. Now it had become the waiting room for the bugs. They get transferred at the end to a receiver strung off the mooring line, which is like a large trap, but with floats to keep it on the surface.

The line on the trap told my fingers of its age and of its worries. I gave it more slack in compensation. It would not be under strain, then, not until I had to pull it. And the next time I pull it, there will be a fresh coil of propylene line waiting on deck. And it will be on deck because I have still the West End to fish, and the West End will be loaded. Line is not very expensive. This old mossy stuff has only to hang on for a few more days. Maybe because the line is old, I lost so many of the others. New line could have changed that, and line is quite cheap. One or two good days.

How could I have slept so long?

From a delta-shaped inlet I pulled another trap. Nothing staggering. One or two lobsters. Both males. The wind was turning into stone, and I could feel the sluggish drag under the hull. A few hundred more rpms for maneuverability. Had I checked the fuel last evening?

I had forgotten. I am sure that there is enough. I haven't changed the filters in two months.

Long overdue.

Another trap ahead.

I don't think I have missed any, lost any, on this stretch of the Island. Not too turbulent here. I positioned the boat, and soon the whining of the winch distracted me.

Rust attacked it like sand flies attacking rotting kelp. A bit of oil for it. Or a new one next season. The line that was gathering on it was fraying. But I shall be wise, this time. I'll keep this trap on the stern deck. Tomorrow, or the day after, I will carry into Avalon what the West End will yield.

Then new line.

I-will-not-loose-another-trap.

The winch was straining. Kelp, I thought.

I was wrong.

The trap broke the surface and was clear of seaweed. At a glance I saw eight or ten lobsters, but the same glance told me that only two of them were large enough to sell.

I pulled out from the island, a bit, before attending to the trap, for the wind gave us a drift, now, and I was working perilously close to the shore. The tide was a storm-high, and that obscured some of the rocks that were generally awash when I fish. I had a deep draft, and with the right combination of swells, I could be over a pinnacle, and have a hole punched in me.

Out from the island, then, and upwind.

I took another look at the line, and then a quick survey of the sky. There was no indication of storm. If there is not much agitation, if I give plenty of slack, I can plant this one again, chance it with the old line. Chance it with the old line so that I can buy a new line. A good spot. These are too small, but there must be some bulls down there. A good facing on the cliffs, too. Lots of erosion, slides. That meant a rocky bottom. That meant protected areas for the lobsters, to attract them. I decided to dump the trap again.

New line, the next time, I vowed.

Melissa took the helm. I unscrewed the plug over the fuel tanks. I pulled the dip-stick, and it looked as if I had a quarter of a tank, but that was deceiving. The way this boat of mine rolls the fuel is always sloshing in the drums. Christ. I should go around and fill at the Twin Harbors, the lee side of the isthmus. Not enough time today. After the West End. Tomorrow. If there is less than a quarter of a tank, I might not have enough. I replaced the cap, and rejoined Melissa. Instinctively, I dropped the rpms. It just drinks up too much that way.

My face was drawn tight, cinched shut like a sail bag. My muscles cinched together. I passed a point that I knew had two of my traps. They could not be found. Melissa looked at me knowingly. She remembered, too, but said nothing. But of course, I did not give her the opportunity.

Goats on the cliffs chewing grass dispassionately.

I realized that there were not many more traps before I hit the West End. The West End is completely exposed, but there is a long stretch of shallow water that extends far from the island. I don't think I will have lost any there. But today it's out of the question. The wind. The sea and the hour. There may not even be light when we enter the harbor. It can be cold, returning that way.

My next trap. I was upon it.

Because there are very few traps left, now, there *must* be a half a dozen lobsters in this one. That many will get me fuel tomorrow, or whenever it is that I fuel up.

A half a dozen, and it can't storm in the morning. The winch was turning, and I tried to ignore the inharmonious meshing of its gears.

Very much rust. Tonight I will dismantle that and oil it. But this trap, the one I am bringing to the surface, it must be full. It must be full. Because its emptiness might fill me.

Its emptiness did.

I pulled from the cove. The rpms, too many. But I burned myself with the last trap. So, away from it, so more rpms. The next trap. I found it, though the buoy was not there where I had planted it. It could mean a number of things. Maybe it migrated with the storm tides. Or maybe somebody else emptied it for me.

I nudged up to it, but was blown off before I could get to the deck. I nudged up again, and held the bow to the wind for a moment. The gust stopped, and I hustled to the deck and the gaff, giving the wheel to Melissa. I snared the float. I gathered in some line by hand, and fed it to the winch. The winch was groaning, really, chewing in the line like a lobster chewing kelp. I let out a little slack. I tugged on the line myself, for interpretation. Oh no! It is under the ledge, or something. I pulled and knew it was stuck and not just heavy. I gave it slack, and walked forward to the bow with it. I pulled again, but it was a wasted effort.

"How deep?" I shouted.

"About thirty feet."

I cast the line free from the boat.

I'll have to get it with a grappling hook, when the water settles down. I couldn't pull it. Maybe the winch could have done it, but the line is thin and the line is old. I can't lose another trap. I'd snap it for sure. I just hope to hell I'm not going to be pulling up a cage full of skeletons.

Six or eight more traps, I think.

I was on the next one. Melissa did what she could to hold the boat to the wind, to hold it in place, but as I pulled in the float, I could hear a sputtering sound, the Diesel's death rattle.

I dropped the float, and flung open the engine hatch. I slipped, on the oil I think, I fell against the engine, and rolled off it, and my hand grasped the reserve valve. I was on my knees in the oily bilge, but thank god I caught it in time. The engine surged again as it was getting fuel from the reserve system. The little clear canister in the fuel line filled again, but it was like turning over an hour glass.

Slimy now, my jeans soaked and my face spattered, I pulled myself out of the bilge, and dropped the hatch. I should really pump out that fucking bilge. That's what's slowing me down, not just the wind. Do that tonight. Or maybe on the way back. I emptied my boots over the rail, as Melissa took us out of the little cove. My hair was holding the oil like guilt and all I could smell were the Diesel fumes.

I slipped my feet into the boots again.

I could not even smell the rancid dead fish that seemed to serve so ineffectively as bait. Bait in the next trap. The empty trap. I don't understand this. It should have been loaded.

We brought the beast of a boat on to the next float.

A good little pocket, out of the wind and the main current. Good. I can use the rest. I pulled the trap, to the sound of the winch which was coming across increasingly suspect, unreliable.

The trap was empty.

I dumped it, with new bait.

I hit the next trap, the winch grinding. The trap was on the surface. I pulled it over the rail.

The trap was empty.

I put fresh bait in it. I launched it. We pulled up to the next trap. Cranked it to the surface.

It was empty.

Desperately, I looked at Melissa. I motioned her to take the boat forward. Away, away from all this. Oh shit. I launched it forgetting to bait it. I looked hurriedly to the helm to see that Melissa did not notice. Gulls were silhouettes on the sun now, a few more hours of light, I think. We edged into the last cove before the West End. I wanted to be finished, and in the harbor. My clothes held the dampness to me. Another pair of jeans below, I think. No matter, only three or four more traps left today, and then we can go home.

I hope to hell I've got enough fuel to work tomorrow. Maybe leave the harbor at four. Be around the other side for fuel when they open. By eight o'clock back to the West End. Finish checking the traps I baited yesterday. I'll have to see. I'll just have to wait and see.
Little sparks. Like little sparks of flame, the granite on the hill with the sun on them.

I hauled a float into me. I fed it to the winch, which I now completely distrusted. I depressed the switch, and it responded with the slow, slow grinding. I could see an indistinct cage coming up, but it didn't really matter. The winch, I mean, being undependable.

The trap was empty.

I set it on the deck. I'll drop it on the West End. I just want to get out of here. I am feeling so cold. My damp clothes, and I could feel the Diesel oil crawling on my legs, and my arm stinging. I burned it on the manifold when I slipped in the bilge, but there is later for that. My hands, tired, doing work on another trap. We were on another trap, going to each one like looking for shelter from a storm, and being consistently refused. We were on another trap.

I took the line to the winch, and depressed the button. It was coming slowly. Could mean it's full, or could mean it's twisted up in eel grass or kelp. Probably kelp. Too deep for eel grass here. But it could mean that it's really full. Otherwise, have to pull the West End before I go around. I'll fuel up tomorrow when they open if this is full. It could really be full.

I had no way of knowing. It was really straining. Could be that the gears are worn on the winch, or that it needs oil. I don't know, but at least it was moving, coming up.

Then there was mild surge ... and the line snapped.

I never saw the trap. The line snapped and the trap was gone.

I don't understand. I don't understand.

The Diesel oil was just crawling over my skin, like a centipede of glue.

I don't understand.

I examined the line, the line that was too old, and I pretended to be surprised by that discovery. It was splintered on every braid. I'll have to come back with a hook. Find it when the water clears. It seemed that even the Diesel engine was moved to show a little compassion, because as I mounted the bridge and took the helm, I don't think I even heard it, couldn't hear the throbbing and pounding of the gray beast.

Two more traps, now. Two more traps and I can go home.

On the small of my back, under the sweater and shirt, Melissa's tiny hand. She had kept it buried under her sweater for at least ten minutes, making it warm for me against her skin. On my back, now, as I took the helm. Thank you. Thank you more than you will ever know. But it's not over yet. There are two more traps. Two more defeats before we can return. And then, in the morning, there is the West End. I will not miss it. I don't know how I could have slept so late, but tomorrow I will not miss it. Tonight, there may not even be sleep. I will not fail you in the morning. So, perhaps one more sleepless night. There have been so many this winter but this shall be the last. God, I can't imagine this oily body of mine even getting close to you, your skin, Melissa.

I reached back and took her hand. I did not care to look at it. I know what my hands look like, so rough. I do not even want to see them framing hers. I wrapped her hand around the spoke of the wheel. We were in place for me to pull another trap.

"Hold it there," I said.

Pull the trap, I thought to myself as I descended the ladder.

I took the line over the pulley on the rail. I started the winch. One, two revolutions, not more. And then it seized, seized up tight.

Rust.

I should have oiled it. Rust in the bearings or cogs or something. I don't know. I should have attended to that while I was stormed in.

But of course, while I was stormed in and it was not in operation, I could not hear the grinding to warn me to attend it. No matter, at least I have a bit of cleaning oil, cutting oil, and I'll do it tonight, in the harbor. It shall be a long night anyway, because I will not sleep. That's decided now, now with the winch. I can fix it then. Only have to take it apart with a few wrenches, and oil it. Thank god it didn't happen sooner. It could have happened at the beginning. Only two traps now, pull them. This one and one other. I took my hands and wrapped them over the slime covered line. I started to pull. Losing my grip. The line was slipping from me, the wind was picking up.

"More throttle," I said.

"What?"

"More throttle!" I had to scream it at her. The water and wind, cannon and shrapnel. Melissa responded, holding the boat in place, holding the bow to the face of the wind. One at a time, I shook my gloves off and dropped them behind me, and I had traction on the line for it, the line trenching itself into my hands. Only two traps. I can manage that by hand.

The trap was surfaced. With my chest on the rail I paused to breath. The trap was heavy, and I could not inhale deeply. I gathered my strength, could feel it gather in my shoulders and arms. I heaved, succeeding in pulling it halfway out of the water. A strand of kelp holding the bottom, no doubt. One big effort now, that's all.

I pulled again.

My rubber boots, the slippery decks, I slid. I slid and fell to the deck, my back catching a corner of the fish-hold. The trap, empty, lay dead beside me. One to go, just one.

Pull the trap.

Feel no pain, I told myself. A rib, I think. Not broken, surely, but sore. I lowered my head, hiding my face from Melissa. Melissa, I love you. Why does that not make all this easier? Just one more trap and it's over, finished for today.

No, that's not right. When I get to the harbor, there is work, work to be done. The bilges, remember? And the winch. And maybe even siphoning some fuel from another boat. They'll take what I've got in exchange, surely. The lobsters, I mean. Save going around to the other side.

Pull the next fucking trap.

Even thinking about the harbor gave me no comfort.

I gathered my hands to my face, as if adjusting my watch-cap, and I sat up. Something. I've done something to my back. Just one more trap. I stood. Then, ignoring my body, I mounted the helm and firmly took the wheel.

"It's alright," I said. Melissa peeling away my shirt to examine my back. She conceded that it was, for of course, it had not yet swelled or turned blue.

The last trap.

The boat in position for it.

The wind pulling at my skin, pulling my face into old age.

—~~— NINE —~~—

Melissa, can you forgive me for what I am thinking now?

I mean, if you knew, would you forgive me for what I am thinking now? I am not thinking of the right things. I am not thinking of the next trap, I am not thinking of a way out of all this.

I am thinking about our son.

That little stretch of beach we saw by the last trap. That started it. It makes me think of the sand spit back by the harbor. And the sand spit makes a very small cove where a fine silt has collected and the water is never very agitated. Someday we will have a boy, and he will toss stones on the mud-flats to see the clams spouting where the stones fall. And then, Melissa, with his small hands, with his small shovel, the kind of shovel that most little boys have for playing in a sandbox, he will dig down into the mystery of mud and he'll find a clam, no clams, dozens of them! As the day wears, his muddied hands will turn them over like pearls, but of far more worth than pearls. He stares at them in wonder, and his little green sand pail will fill.

That will be a day, Melissa, he shall feel his own hands, power still pure, virtuous, not tainted by doubt, and oblivious to fear. He will with his own power find food, and eat, and survive. I will teach him that. He will rescue a day from defeat before he even will know what defeat means. He will take his own meal from the mud, mud filtered pure by the sea, and stored in the cove, layer upon layer to keep the clams for him, till he finds them. A legacy from the sea to him. He's going to squat down and find clams and I swear to you he shows me each and every one, and each time the same wonder in his eyes, that clams, which he has seen before, not knowing from where they come, can be found in the mud, and that he, himself, can find them.

That morning will be exclusively ours, Melissa, his and mine. I shall look down at my son—no, not down on him—I shall kneel down in the mud beside him as he shows me the work that he has done, and I shall say "That's good!" and he smiles, so proud. Like god, only kinder, I shall say to him "That's good!"

And then he shall feel my strength. I shall lift him and stand, and walk across the mud, for his legs are tired and would strain in the mire. Mine strain too, but I carry him, three years old, perhaps, his head on my shoulder, mud-oozing between his bare chest and mine, bonding us, almost, and he looks down over my shoulder to his little bucket and it is swinging on my back like a bo's'ains chair on a mast, and he sees the clams, he sees what he has done.

I walk. He is bundled into me, I, looking forward to the boat on its mooring, home, he looking back to the mud-flats, his victory. A moistness, like the mud but cooler, I feel upon my neck.

He has kissed me … .

I must tell you this Melissa, I must. I want to tell you. Can you forgive me for thinking this now, for thinking this when I should be thinking of, of … yes, thinking of the trap.

Pull the trap and I can head home.

The harbor.

Home.

Home.

The sound of the Diesel pouring into me, flooding into me, flooding into me and drowning everything, drowning all my senses and yet still, miraculously, am I breathing. The thought of the sand spit, the little cove, washed out, and I moved the throttle forward like opening the flood gates, and the sound intensified and surged in me.

I gasped, as if for breath. I must hold my breath a little while longer though, just a little while longer. Just one more trap.

Then, a renegade thought. What if the last trap is not there?

Other boats, I could see them returning.

Melissa, you know sometimes I get the urge to leave all this? I mean, just leave it, the boat on its mooring, and go to Canada or something. Just hitch-hike till I find a quiet little town, get a job washing dishes in some truck-stop cafe, where I've got a room in the back to stay. I mean, sometimes I think that. And I think of leaving you, too, you, who are the witness to failures to my fictional self.

I wonder, when did you first come to recognize that I am not fearless? I must redeem myself, Melissa, before what you must surely know deep inside floats up to your cool surfaces and you recognize me for the coward that I am. And, as a coward, I fear that you will make that discovery. A race, then, to redeem myself before that happens.

You who I love are the witness to my daily defeats and I hate you for it. I slept with that woman because you deserve better than me. How else could I prove it?

Even mild success cannot insulate me from the knowledge of my own failing. Even if I become wrapped in success now, I cannot ignore my own shivering defeat. Melissa, the truth is, I'm freezing. Thank god there is just one trap left. One mother-fucking trap.

Oh, and something else, Melissa, while I'm being honest with you. Do you know that I swear, when I think to myself? Of course you don't.

Thank god, a float. The last trap.

Melissa, for what it's worth … I love you.

But I know what it's worth.

Gulls, a tribunal, witnessed my approach to the last trap. It crossed my mind that somehow, at one time, before stress bent me into what I thought I would never become, I was disciplined enough to insure the boat against loss or destruction. I had taken out a policy.

I look at you, what all this has done to you and I feel like torn sail. I swear I hear my dream being ripped like sail to the wind and the wind blows through me like I am torn and I just can't fill myself like I used to. Somewhere else would be nice; I really do think of leaving. But then this dream, the one that is so rapidly awakening, will become my harbor. This place, these years, a harbor to which I return. And each new ocean flows from this harbor. It will always be, again and always, back to Catalina. And the hair gets long and the clothes wear thin and are even discarded in the noon-day sun, and the beard gets bleached and the skin gets bronzed and the hands swell thick with pains but the pains turn fast to calluses, and the birds fly low and the swells lie low and the sea is clear and the traps are full, the traps are full and it's Avalon on weekends and feeding pigeons and reading books in the shade of the woods overlooking the beach, and other things, other things, too …

… But the traps are empty … the traps have been empty, and that awakens me. A dream cannot be salvaged with a grappling hook.

There is this one last trap, and if it is full, the dream falls deeper into sleep and safety, for sleep is the harbor for my dreams to which they can return.

The trap, this last one, has only to be full.

These things that I think distract me from myself. I am not thinking, really, of how to maneuver this boat, when to cut, when to slow down, but somehow all that is done, and here I am, with three gulls staring at me from the water.

I took the splintery gaff; I snagged the float. As I pulled it to me, my back throbbed from the fall of a few moments before. I took the float, and I dropped the gaff on the deck behind me.

I gripped the line, and I started to take in the last trap of the day. I hated doing it without gloves, but with gloves it could not have been done. Too slippery. Anyway, one of the gloves was missing. It must have washed over.

The line became taught, was straining, and so was my back, and then a mild gust of wind started pushing the bow out, and the trap on the bottom was like an anchor, and I was a link in the chain that held the boat in position. The drift intensified, and I felt my arms straining, could almost hear them straining like hemp or manila and the thin yellow line was slipping through my palms, slipping through until the sting of my hand and the bite of my back had me dropping it all, all that I had succeeded in gathering, dropping it over the rail, before I got a turn on the cleat.

Up to the helm again. I wish I had given Melissa more time at the wheel over the last few months. She could have handled it, kept us from drifting. I took the boat in a very broad circle, the gulls accommodating me, taking to the sky. Does that qualify itself as a defeat, Melissa? And, if that is defeat, does that not entitle me to head for the harbor, now? Silent, and the wind revealing her face and scattering her hair, her sullen face.

I made another approach to the trap, holding the boat in place until I sensed that gust had passed, and Melissa's hair, like a telltale on a stay, settled gently on her shoulders, lightly.

All things should touch you lightly, Melissa, as once I did. You are a better woman than I am a man, because you can love without feeling desire.

I took to the deck and the gaff.

The float was in my hands again, and this time the slack came with no interference from the wind, and soon I was directly over the trap, the line vertical beneath me. No, something wrong. I am not lifting the trap suspended somewhere below me. It is I who am suspended, over the edge of the world, and this line is all I have.

Slowly, I inched my hands along the yellow cord, pulling myself from defeat. I have only to pull this trap, and its only obligation is to be full, and I can return. My arms, my back, a barometer sensing victory or humiliation by the weight of that upon which I pulled.

It's heavy!

God it's heavy! Is that just my back, the ache, or is it really that full? It could be snagged in the kelp. "Melissa!"

She came, almost before I called, and then her hands were taking in line, too.

"Get a turn on the cleat." She took the slack line and secured it, as I held in the tension. I paused for a moment and my face contorted to the twisting in my back, but Melissa did not see. If you could see my face, would you be following the lines? They are slicing my forehead, cutting deep and eroding my face. I am aging.

I tested the line again, but had no way of knowing if the strain on the line was because the trap was full, or because it was stuck. Maybe both. I glanced at the winch. I should really have taken it apart at the harbor and oiled it.

Mild swells again. If the trap were caught under a canopy of kelp, the rising of the boat with the swells would break it free, but if instead it were under a ledge, having shifted during the storm, the rising would snap the line. I could not have that, and yet I was tempted to hesitate to see which would give first.

No, I can't have that.

I pulled the line away from the boat and with all the strength in my arms acted as shock cord to keep the swells from rocking the line until it snapped from tension or from chaffing on the rail. It would not have been the first trap lost that way.

But, when the swells gave no indication of dying, and my arms began to burn, I dropped the line, and loomed over the winch, wishing I had a club.

I uncleated the line with Melissa's help and tossed the float for a second time into the water, and took the helm again. Not to the open water this time, but to a corner of the cove I maneuvered the boat, for I decided to-fix the winch, right then and there, and pull the trap.

Let the sun set, if it will. It doesn't matter since there will be no sleep tonight anyway. I will not lose this one. I will not.

I pointed the bow out, and kicked off the hook. I backed down until I could feel I was caught good. The anchor dug in deep, but this close to shore it was best that it did. A drag this close to the rocks could complicate things.

Of course, it is not the winch that is the conspirator. It is you and me, Melissa. We conspire to deceive ourselves that what is empty should be full, simply because we will it, or work for it. Empty traps incriminate me, and I fear to pull them, to have their testimony.

I will fix this winch. I have only to tolerate this insanity a half an hour longer than I had originally thought. It can't take longer than that.

I explained what I had planned to Melissa. Reward me, Melissa. God knows, you know how. But then, after I committed myself, I realized that I had no oil. In fact, that is why the bilges are so oily. The can of cutting oil tipped over in some heavy swells a few weeks ago. Jesus, how could I have forgotten?

Oil. Of course I have oil!

I went below for a coffee cup. Crack in the porcelain anyway, need a new one. Ingenious, I thought. I would drain just a little oil, about half a cup, from the engine. A half a cup would not make that much difference. It would be dirty, but it would work until a few good days of fishing changed things. Then fresh oil. Fresh everything.

I slid back the hatch, and wormed my way beside the engine. What a hideous sound. The sloshing in the bilge and the grumbling. Shit. Damn near enough oil in the bilge to lubricate the winch. I braced myself against one of the members, the engine being hot, and I could still feel the boat rolling a bit. I reached down under the crankcase and found the thumbscrew. Good. Not below the water mark. This small success even helping me forget that I am not in the harbor.

I took the cap and unscrewed it, shot the cup down to the spigot and oil gushed out thick and dark, and I panicked to think that this was the stuff I had lubricating the engine. It's a wonder the engine didn't seize from it. One or two good days of fishing. I've got to get new oil.

Then, a swell again, a severe one.

I was surged towards the engine and its heat. I instinctively threw out my right hand in defense and caught a support, my left hand miraculously balancing the oil cup. But I had dropped the screw, and oil, life, was bleeding from the engine!

I recovered my balance, and stabbed into the bilge water desperately for the screw, the oil gushing over my forearm.

Nowhere! Nowhere to be found! I stuck my thumb up into the wound and the oil stopped. I called at once for Melissa, and handed her the cup of oil, before another swell might cause me to drop even that.

With a polluted hand I reached down into my pocket and pulled out a handkerchief. It would have to do. I wadded it up as best I could with my free hand, and jammed it into the hole in the dike. My hands were oiled beyond recognition, but were unburned. My forehead was feeling the heat and I crawled out of the hold and up on the deck. We were anchored. There were, of course, imperatives, but we were anchored. I laid on the hard wet deck and it seemed so soft and warm. But the sight of Melissa standing over me like a gladiator stopped that. She was looking somehow like a gladiator over me. I sat up, my legs dangling in the hold, and with enough fresh air to be recovered, I crawled down into the hold again, for the tools.

I looked at the oil pressure gauge that was mounted directly on the engine. Lower, much lower than before the spill. And it had been low to begin with. I should not have done it, but if I can handle just a few more days, I'm sure not more than just a few more days, I can replace the oil. Run it a little slower, that's all.

I saw the oil dripping, a painful drop at a time, from the handkerchief that served as a plug. Just a few more hours. It has only to hold for a few more hours. Then I shall be back in the harbor and can pump the bilge dry. And when that is done, I will surely find the thumbscrew that I dropped. Just a few more hours.

Yet, a few more hours frightened me. The boat had been running with too little oil, and the oil that I did have in it was old. The cup-full showed me that, testified as to the state of my poverty. If the Gray Marine gets hot, too hot, I could burn the rings, scorch the pistons. Like the last time.

Achh! Later for that. I have come for the tools, to take down the winch. I crawled back to the trunk, in which I kept a small case of tools, good tools, my wrenches there. I needed them. I opened the trunk.

Like pulling a TRAP! "Ahh!" I opened the trunk and it was empty!

Empty, empty!

The tools! The day before, while at Avalon, stolen! Stolen. The same word for a spectrum of feelings. Stolen! Anger.

Stolen! Shock and disbelief.

Stolen! Frustration and I twisted my fingers around themselves, like a cripple.

Stolen. I pounded a beam with the fleshy part of my fist.

NO! Stolen! Contempt.

Stolen. Stolen and at last the word meant resignation. Stolen. I looked up with shame at Melissa. "Stolen," I said, confessed.

I left the engine hold, and I slid the engine hatch in place. I mounted the helm, where Melissa had gone to escape the fumes. "They've been stolen," I said, in a please-pass-the-mashed-potatoes kind of voice, and I waited modestly for her to say that it wasn't my fault, which she compliantly did for me, though, as I think of it, I had to prompt her to do that. "It's all my fault," I said.

"No, it's not," she said. Something like that that left me feeling so alone. Melissa went down below to get out of the cold, for the sun, though not yet setting, was behind a pinnacle and in the shadow, it was quite cold really. It is really quite cold, and that is why she had to go below, I told myself.

I paused a moment, and my body accommodated my little rationale and even shivered for me once. It is really quite cold, and she had to go below. I looked at the gauges on the panel of the bridge.

I walked to the bow, to take in the anchor. The wind, though blowing into me, was not a handicap, as I had dropped the hook in the protection of a cliff that filtered the wind.

I was vertical, I mean, I was right over the anchor and I pulled with my defeated arms, but the anchor was fast. Of course. It's a rocky area, bound to be tight. No problem. Muscle it out with the boat. I went back to the wheel while Melissa was still somewhere below, and I throttled the Monterey boat forward. Good quarter inch chain.

The boat eased forward, until I could feel the strain that vibrated through the hull like a warning. It was tight. I throttled back, hoping I had broken something loose, but the bow of the boat did not flow with the rhythm of the swells, meaning that it was holding tight to the bottom. The line was taught leading from the bitt to the chock, and from the chock to water. I could not bend it.

I let out slack, and pulled up on it again, but I was well hooked. I left a bit of slack, and took the wheel again, and I pivoted from the anchor, forcing the stern to seaward, and after putting the gears in neutral, I was down to the foredeck again, carrying with me a remembrance of the disastrously low oil pressure and a correspondingly high rise in temperature of both oil and water.

I tried the hook again, before the stern was blown around, but it was stuck. I looked to the vacated helm. If Melissa were only there to help me … . No, there is nothing that she can do there. I dismissed it. I examined the line, to reassure myself of its strength.

I went back to the wheel, this time determined to push the old Monterey boat until the chain on the line broke up the rocks that entangled it. It can't be just the hook that's holding me. Pull from the last trap showed me I had a rocky bottom here, but sandstone. Soft stuff. I should be able to break free with enough tension. Just put it on slow, though hard, to keep any sudden jerks from snapping the line.

I edged forward, and it held, which increased my confidence in the line through the chock, but it made the bottom seem so much more formidable. I released more throttle, but the boat surged against the line and nothing more.

Drop this. It's not going to work. I even had visions of the line snapping, like the line from the lobster trap I had previously severed.

I had experienced this before, it was nothing strange. But at the other times, when I couldn't pull the anchor, I fed the line to the lobster winch and the slow and steady tension always did it for me, always broke me free. But of course, I was anchored here precisely because the winch was broken. I imagined spending the night at this anchorage. I just wanted to go below. But it was a dangerous anchorage even under mild conditions, and the outgoing tide brought the wash-rocks that much closer to the surface.

I went instead to the lazurette, and pulled out a few musty life-jackets. I tied them together, and then secured them to the anchor line. The wind was picking up; I had no choice but to ask Melissa's help. I knocked politely on the hatch, and as she opened it, I looked sheepishly to the helm, and she understood that she was needed. She took the helm, just as a precaution, as we were close to shore on a windward side, and as Melissa witnessed the act, I cast the anchor free and we were adrift. Two life jackets bundled together as if for warmth marked the spot to which I would return when I fixed the winch, when I had just a few good days of fishing under my belt.

Melissa did not ask what I would do if the engine stopped this close to shore now that I had no anchor. The other two anchors, the spares, had been traded for fuel and for credit at the settlement, months before, when it first started to get a bit rough for us. This boat is a fugitive, carrying too much and discarding the excess a little at a time. The anchors, the traps, sold.

I looked back at the life jackets gasping for air, abandoned and having to fend for themselves. Do not dwell on their fate, I thought. Do not dwell on my own.

The last trap. Jesus, it had felt heavy. Its weight still recorded in my arms and back. It must be loaded. No, that is a lie.

I know it is really not loaded. It was too secured, too tight. Under a ledge, like the hook and chain. What the fuck was I doing with a Danforth here anyway? A little grappling hook would have been better. In fact, might not even have gotten stuck.

A grappling hook. That's what I need. All the traps that I have to find when the water settles and clears. Snag them with a grappling hook. But, I have to fish a few good days, first, because even the grappling hook is no longer my property. Sold for fuel or traded for traps or something. I have forgotten. No, I have not forgotten. That, again, is a lie, but it has been a very successful lie for me. Fished all day thinking that I had a grappling hook.

Well, when the water clears, after I fish the West End, I will have enough for a grappling hook. The West End should really be loaded. I hope nobody sees the life jackets; it's an invitation to a new larceny.

Is that a lie too, the West End being loaded? I must deceive myself a while longer.

I was soon away from the cove, and could see the sun full and round and considering going down. Birds, not knowing any better, trailed me as if I would throw them scraps. They dropped to the water like over-ripened fruit as the boat churned up foam, but came away empty.

I looked to them sadly. *It's not like that,* I said. *If I had it, I would give it to you,* the entrails of fish or abalone that bait the traps. They were tired as I, but they followed. A bit higher and they could have caught the currents to carry them ahead of me back to the harbor, yet they persisted, sometimes dropping behind a bit, sometimes trotting ahead of me like hunting dogs accompanying a horseman back to the stables.

"But I have nothing," I said, out loud, "and it should have been easy for you today." I balanced the wheel as best I could. It was a stiff wheel, and I set a course to Cat Head, directly to Cat Head. The birds, I could not ignore them.

I came down to the deck, and was so tired that I was not even quickened by the anxiety that comes from leaving the wheel unattended. But the birds. I am not akin to the fishermen in the harbor, I know that, and I have no compassion for their suffering ... but the birds. They looked so abused. In the fish-hold in a damp burlap bag I had small abalone pried from the rocks a few days before, to use as bait when the dead fish became too stale to have the scent that attracts lobsters. They were small and tough, blacks, and not the most palatable kind, yet I thought that I might even eat them myself. They can be good, boiled, a squeeze of lemon. I lifted one out and pulled it from its shell and on the transom I hacked it into several pieces, and flung each piece high into the air and the gulls took it. I looked to see if Melissa had come out yet, but the hatch was still secured. It was getting a bit cold. I did not want her to see me feeding the gulls, giving away the bait. I begged the gulls to take it, but to keep their silence and to tell no one where they had taken the food, to join me in that plot so Melissa wouldn't hear. Be silent, but know that I understand.

The gulls disobeyed me, and as they took the last of the abalone, they began to cry, and I quickly mounted the helm for an alibi should the cries have brought Melissa from the cabin.

She must be sleeping. I hope she is sleeping. Because, if she is sleeping, she is not condemning me for this, all that has happened today.

I miss the old gull, the one that used to eat the pancakes in the morning, walk across the stern of the boat as if he owned it.

The water before me was made of oak, it was thick and hard and I had such a long way to cut with the dull teeth of the prop before I could be in the harbor. The sun was at eye level and as such it made the brown-gold color on Cat Head that always seems so warm at this time of day in spite of the wind. Yes, the wind is picking up. It is going to get colder, but once I get around Cat Head, I can bury the boat in its shoulder like a bird burying its head under a wing. Cat Head, just a little while longer.

No, that is—among other things I have felt and done today—just not true. It is not just a little while longer.

It is at least another hour before I will be inside the harbor. Swells seeming to aid me, rolling me towards the harbor, but it is distant, never-the-less. The wind going with me, but I have to pay for that, it's cold and it's sapping the heat from me.

I looked and saw that there were no longer any birds against the sun, yet I don't recall their passing. They must be in the harbor and I am envious. But wait, that's right, it doesn't matter, because tonight there will be no sleep. That was my declaration. No sleep. It has nothing to do with the work to be done, though the work to be done is my reason for not sleeping tonight. It is my punishment to myself for being a failure today, sentence myself to sleeplessness. No, now that is too noble. It is my attempt to manipulate God with a guilt feeling. The way He does it to Christians. God, look at the abuse I am suffering. Do you not honestly think I should be compensated? Fill the traps, you Fucker. Fill the traps and I shall pull them.

The sun, flattening against the water. A silhouette or two of birds that are not gulls across the sun, what is left of it. Indistinct. I remember falling asleep as a tiny boy in the back of a station wagon, on the long trips home, and waking just enough to feel my father's arms carrying me to bed, and the sheets were cool and clean and he was a silhouette against the light in the hall.

I smiled to welcome the harmless fantasy of falling asleep and awakening in the harbor, as if carried there. But now, I carry Melissa there, and someday a baby .... I dozed at the wheel yet the breaking of the rhythm of the swells was enough to jar me. What was I thinking, I have forgotten. Oh yes, silhouettes, something about silhouettes. The birds, against the sun.

Yet I looked over my shoulder, and the sky was empty. The sky, empty like the traps.

Going from bar to bar, looking for the right woman, but always coming up empty. So many times just empty. But there is not the emptiness with Melissa, things to work out, but not emptiness with her, because, if there is not Melissa, what could draw me out again?

The sound of the Diesel was throbbing and numbing. I felt like an army wife, maybe twenty-two years old, must feel going to a Laundromat with all the other army wives, together, just getting numb to the drone of the machines turning and turning like my Diesel engine, vaguely aware that they can go home. The drone making the time shorter, hypnotic.

The hypnotic drone of the Diesel. More than distracting, hypnotic. I did not see the kelp.

The blade caught the first fronds of a paddy of kelp that was broken loose and ostracized by the storm, a large paddy, and as it took the prop, the rpms dropped and the spell was broken and I was wide awake and alert at once, and my eyes flashed quickly to the panel. Kelp, like barbed wire, was choking the prop, and in a moment, the engine had stopped.

It brought Melissa from below.

She came charging from below to the helm. "Why didn't you go around it? Didn't you see it?" She had the frantic look of disbelief. Surfacing. Your contempt for me is surfacing and soon you will be fully aware of it.

"Melissa, you know the other night, a week ago, when you said I was so passionate, when I had all that energy and I surged in you, I mean I just surged in you and it was so intense?"

She looked at me dumbfounded.

"Well, you know what it was? I was pretending that I was giving you a baby. That's what did it."

Jesus, she took it so bad.

We were adrift, and the chance of getting the boat started again was minimal, and anyway, we were fast to the kelp. No, she did not understand, of course not. She had come up on deck without a jacket, and the wind was so cold. She went below, retreated from me.

I, too, abandoned the helm. I took to the deck and could see the West End behind me. Tomorrow, if there is nothing there, it's over. The sky still had some color to it, working overtime, like me. Melissa came from below again, and in spite of a sweater looked cold. I took off my sweater as if to give it to her. When she did not reach for it, I dropped it to the deck.

I began to unbutton my shirt.

"What, what are you doing?"

"I am taking off my clothes," I said. "Is that not obvious?" She gathered my clothes as they fell. The wind took to my back like flame takes to a fresh spar. I turned away from her, facing the West End and I unfastened my jeans and pulled off my boots. I began to shiver. I dropped my jeans to the damp deck. The kelp, it had to be cut. I scanned the deck, and saw the machete, and my attraction to it was at once a new experience, like learning to walk, but devious. I dropped cat-like to the deck, and my hand grew to the sword like a vine on a wall, and my hand pulled it to within my power. I grinned with proud degeneration as I felt it within my fingers, the hand fusing to it until the difference between the two became indistinguishable. My shoulders broadened and strengthened, and the muscles of my arm spiraled to the hand that became a fist, the fist that was tensing around the handle of a blade, and the blade awaiting flight, and my muscles, all of them, hardening to the wind and the cold.

I picked myself up in my nakedness from the deck, facing the stern, facing the wind and the West End. My eyes were swelling with criminal desire, and the sword in my hand pointing the way. Slowly, deliberately, I lifted the blade above me, and I felt the bite of the wind again, but then, leering, knowing what it would do, I turned the blade to the wind, and I heard it scream as it impaled itself.

And suddenly, *I* was the aggressor. The wind screaming past me, my hair like a wheat field through which it retreated, bending every stalk and I stood tall and erect, and my lips parted in a heathen-like smile and I felt that I was biting the wind, biting and drawing blood.

And I looked at the jaws of the water that threatened me with its cold. It was deep and dark and its cold was like the mouth of the night, an empty and cold night, but I looked again to the blade in my hand, to the blade in my fist. I turned from it and took a few steps back.

"What are you doing!" she said.

I took two running steps and sprung from the transom rail, carrying my machete in my hand and I made my descent upon the water and with my fist, punched a hole in it, and was down and under with a lung full of air. Kelp covered up the place where I entered, surrounding me from above, leaving no escape. 1 opened my eyes but did not blink, and I pulled myself under the hull to the prop and the keel, slicing along the way, cutting and chopping at the kelp indiscriminately, and then finding the shaft of the boat with the kelp tight around it like a noose and I hacked against it.

For a moment, I lost color, the first sign of blacking out. I gulped, and the craving for air stopped. I don't know how long I was down, but I kept cutting and my rage defied my lungs. I cleared enough kelp to see that a strand of yellow propylene line was twisted around the shaft.

Of course, the propylene, torn free, cast out drifting in the storm, leaving a trap somewhere on the bottom and the line to join the kelp that was also cast out, broken loose. Maybe even my own line.

I dove down deeper, as I felt myself becoming entangled in the kelp, and then, seal-like, I surfaced, parting kelp and I took a hungered breath of air, almost biting it, tearing it off like a shark and I took it down with me, to feed on it, and I was at the shaft again, slicing and hacking and then with my free hand, I stabbed at the line and ripped, ripped and it was free, cleared.

Down deeper again, deep and under the kelp, and somehow the feeling to go deeper, and I angled up, beginning to arc and propel myself to the surface and the kelp over me like a web but I was without fear and invincible, and with the machete by my side I broke the surface, I broke the surface and grinned, and took hard and deep the fresh air that awaited me. I turned over on my back to breathe and recover, and then I muscled my way through a few yards of kelp, like coming out of the bush, and my hand took the chine and I hoisted myself up to the rail and boarded my boat. I looked once at the machete, and then dropped it arrogantly to the deck. I ran to the side, looked down to the water again. Impulsively, I picked up the machete and launched it into the kelp like a spear and my accompanying scream was violent and virtuous.

Melissa held my clothes out to me, but I walked past her and took the helm, my helm. I threw my head back and cleared my face of the tangles of hair, and I looked at the panel of terrified instruments before me. I hit the starter button, and in fear of me, the engine started the first time, and I reversed gears and backed out of the kelp, and found a clear path and followed it. Then, then I turned, my whole body, and I spread my stance to make it firm and I looked to the wind and grinned the victor's grin.

I had won. I had won.

There was nothing, absolutely nothing now that could be done to me that was not already done, and yet I still felt, or perhaps for the first time, felt defiant.

I let the wind try my skin. "Do it, go ahead! I can take it! What else can you do to me!" And the wind, broken, spiraling around me, harmlessly, powerlessly, degenerated, falling around me like emptiness, powerless, powerless, I am winning. And in my eyes the West End, the West End. In the morning!

I stood at the ladder, and below me, on the deck, a bewildered woman. I looked at her and grinned, and turned to take my helm again.

And then as I turned my back, a new gust of wind, like a new school of sharks in a frenzy but my skin was just too tough and left them frustrated. I couldn't even feel it. Could not feel their cold teeth. I felt as if the sun were in my body, that I was the source of all warmth. Never was I so aware of my nakedness. Just a few more days of fishing and things will change. I am baptized, water dripping over me like kelp, and Melissa, with a bundle of clothes in her arms, looking at me so plaintively and with such misunderstanding. But don't you see? Don't you understand? That pile of rags in your arms, they're so disgusting, so degrading. *Look at me!* I said, with thoughts so loud they could almost be words. *Look* at this body! Clean and strong and young and swift and invincible ... and *yours*, if you *want* it!

"You must be freezing!" she said. She was close; I was on fire.

I looked to the harbor before me, closer and really not that distant. Just a few more days of fishing and things will be so good. It will be so good here. Just a few good days of fishing. I cast a laugh out before me like a dagger to the heart of whatever god kept me small. I laughed, I laughed, I laughed, I laughed! And then, I avenged myself upon the cruel wind that had taken such pleasure in blowing me off course, or peeling the warmth from my skin. I did not even *permit* my body to shiver, and the wind lost none of its velocity, but all of its power. I willed myself warm and dry, could feel the salt upon my skin and it felt so good, and the oil from the bilge was off of me, and the polluted scent of Diesel had retreated from my nostrils and crawled back to the bilge, and there was only the salt, and the sea.

Beside me, a stack of clothes, the tattered uniform of my despair. Before me, the harbor, its features now distinct. Below me with her disbelief, Melissa.

Just a few more days and it will be over. The West End. In the morning, the West End and the traps will be loaded. As the last darkness filled the sky, my left shoulder was to Cat Head, and the boat was taken in, where the wind could not follow, no, dared not follow. In the morning, the West End.

ELEVEN

It was six o'clock-in the morning of a sleepless night.

The sun, like the goats, could be seen grazing on the east ward channels of the isthmus, the lee side. Remarkably, the first taste of air had been a dry one. I had anticipated more bad weather. The gulls had already gone, the hungriest ones at least, and those that had more to lose waited, but eventually, they too stretched their wings under which they hid by night, and departed to sustain their habit of living.

Precariously, we stepped into the skiff.

We drifted from the boat to the landing. I scarcely dipped the oar into the water, a gentle current taking us in. Melissa would spend the day on shore. "Today, I need to fish alone." After yesterday, she wasn't about to fight me on it. According to our seaman-first-class in San Pedro, today is supposed to be flat. And when it is flat, I can handle the boat myself.

And of course, there are not that many traps to handle now. "I'll blow you a kiss from the West End" I said, all I said, but I meant it.

"I'll buy you an orange when I get into town."

I deprived myself of the kiss I wanted to take. That could wait. That could wait till the West End. I left her standing on the dock, and skulled back to the boat. I secured myself with the frayed line, and climbed over the rail, the banister at the stern, and turned to watch her finding her way into the island. Water and land and nothing else between us. Nothing. "I love you," I said softly, almost a thought more than spoken words.

I turned to the helm rather than waiting to see if she had heard or felt.

I stretched, trying to pull the weight from me. I could feel a stiffness in my back, and under my muscles there was a knot from where I had fallen the day before, and it laid underneath my skin like a washrock. I stretched again, this time to explore my tolerance to it. It was painful, but could be tolerated. I must fish today.

I checked the fuel. Enough. At least if the sea stays flat, there is enough. I had traded what I had caught for some fuel from another boat during the night. Not enough to fill the tanks, but when I get a few dollars ahead, I am going to fill them to the hilt, and keep them full, to keep the insides from rusting. The rust could slough into the Diesel, and then it starts all over again, like it did with the oil. It is never fortune that is elusive, just its first few dollars.

Other boats were not yet started. Of course, theirs were much faster than the Monterey boat. They could sit and wait, as a thin layer of chill was peeled from a mid-December morning. I felt the cold steel pipes, the rungs of the ladder leading to the bridge on the cabin top.

I inhaled deeply of the silence, indulging myself, filling myself with it, knowing it was an oasis, knowing that it would soon pass, and by my own hand. Then I broke the trance and the silence, as my thumb depressed the starter. Smoke escaped through the exhaust, but the engine just wheezed. It turned once or twice, and just stopped. The battery, the goddamn battery.

It just didn't have the strength, not on its own. I felt almost like cradling the battery in my arms, and rocking it like a sobbing baby, or a dying one. Just once, I only have to get it started once. It's like hoisting a sail. Up, and then it's over for you, the strain. The wind does the rest. If I can get it started, just get it started. The alternator can charge it from there. Otherwise, I'll have to wait and get jumped by another boat.

I took the helm in my hands, as if mocking myself, guiding a moored boat, and I leaned forward to take the weight off my wounded back. If I reach for the starter button again, and it doesn't pop, it's all over for me. Might be sitting here when Melissa comes back. I paused, like a knot in a fuse. The West End, if I can just fish the West End.

"NO!" I bolted from the wheel, down the ladder, ripped open the cabin door and stumbled inside. I unscrewed the canister of alcohol from the stove. I looked for a rag, and finding none I pulled my sweater over my head and then pulled off my flannel shirt. Stripped to the waist, with my shirt in a stranglehold and the canister under my arm and held to my chest, I lurched out onto the deck, and with my free hand, I flung open the hatch that covered the engine. I tore a patch from my shirt and now that I had a rag, I saturated that rag with alcohol, and I stuffed it into the air intake.

I took a screwdriver and shorted the wire at the appropriate juncture, and the alcohol was sucked into the straining engine. There was the contained explosion, and without any nonsense, the engine started. Black smoke erupted from the exhaust at the stern, but that was soon coughed out. I pulled out the rag, and satisfied myself that I would out-fish this day. I slammed the hatch shut, and I left the rag that had once been my shirt on the deck. I went below, and, the act being done, pulled my sweater over me and walked— marched—to the bow, secured the skiff to the mooring and released the boat as I did.

I inhaled deeply, something that resembled triumph, and I took my place at the wheel. Did I put the alcohol back? I thought a moment. Yes, I did. Not going to make any mistakes today. A full day of fishing. Start with the West End. Just have to pull the traps. I will buy a new shirt. Today will make the difference. It had been calm all night. I know that the lobsters will be hungry. I broke out of the harbor.

The boat was smoking a little. Just cold, I thought. My hands were tight on the wheel, though the ocean for once seemed domesticated. Not a ripple.

I passed the coves that I wished had been be-speckled with my traps. As I passed Lobster Bay, I could see Ribbon Rock protruding like a head stone towards the West End. Its features were becoming distinct too slowly. Moving too slow. Pull the traps. I moved the throttle a notch deeper.

The boat was still smoking and the color darkened.

The sky was cloudless but for that. The fury that morning was in me and not in the sea or sky. I will be cruel today. I shall cast my body from myself and make it my slave. To pull the traps.

Pull the traps. The Diesel beating as if drumming to flush something from the bush. Pull the traps.

It's a flat day. I should be able to hit all of them before noon, before the wind comes, and then when at last it comes, it shall be only to carry me home. Hit all of them and bait them. I had been at this long enough to know how to bait traps, at least. I knew by the smell when the fish were too old to attract lobsters. I had become skillful at finding black abalone at low water and I knew how to cut them just right, just right so they bled for three or four days, catching lobsters all the time.

Of course, the lobsters themselves make the best bait.

That's why the traps are always full after a storm. There may pass some days before you can pull a trap, and a lobster that is trapped too long starves to death, but when he's dead he attracts others. They're cannibals. They feed off him. But then they are trapped, and if the cage isn't pulled, they die, and then more come to feed on them, and so on. Only when the cage rusts through is the cycle broken, only when the trap is somehow broken up, destroyed.

Thank god I am heading for the West End. The traps there have not been pulled in ten days. Three of those days were flat, the last three. They should be stuffed. I must have fifteen or twenty traps there. All were baited with abalone, and of course, have been baited with lobster if the abalone are gone. I will pull the traps there first. Hope that they have not yet been pulled for me.

I have only to pull the traps. If they are full today, I will have broken it, December's choke hold on us. Break the cycle with my own body, like breaking water and being born. Think only now of pulling the traps. When the sun sets, as I have seen it set before, as I know already how to visualize, it will all be over, at the end of the day, all this bullshit and failure.

And something else to think of. If I return and the traps are full, there is Melissa. I can show her. We can plan things again. That would be allowed. Take the pressure off. It ought to put an end too, to the way we have butchered ourselves at night lately. Change all that. The traps have only to be full.

I looked at the deck before me, and imagined a smiling little boy looking up at me, peering over the rail to watch the water turn from blue to white as the boat parts it, but then looking back up to see me guiding the boat, and looking down to him to see that he is safe.

Dolphins dancing in the distance. He sees them too.

I wish I had kissed her on the dock, that moment when we said good-bye. I wish now that I would really have done that. I would like to be carrying that with me. But, I have only to return. I shall not forget my promise, though. I shall blow her a kiss from the West End. I wish I had held her once at the dock. Why does that, why must that, call for courage? I had only the company of the Diesel. I tried not to think about it, but I could not dump the sound. It did not seem healthy, it sounded abnormal from the bridge.

It is too early for the rings to be bad. It smokes because the oil is not clean, I told myself, or the oil is old. Or there is not enough of it. Like the last time.

But today is the day that will make a difference. I will not indulge myself in anything that resembles luxury. After this haul, I advised myself, you will change the oil. You will see that the fuel tanks are topped off. You will caulk the cabin top. You will replace the oars. The traps too. Paint can wait. Wait till summer for that. It is not easy to see the boat ugly like this, to leave its scars unattended. The boat in its agony, crucified to its old age. I hurt with it, for it, and it is tolerable only if I envision its resurrection. I want to put it on the weighs, heal it with my own hands and roll it down to the sea again, roil away the stone in front of its grave. But that is a comfort only for the eye, the paint, that is. A luxury. Go without paint. Buy one new trap instead of a gallon of paint. Paint. Fuck it.

Ground swells were light and seagulls trailed me optimistically. The water, even the island, had a blueness about it. The air, too, of course, but for the smoke that the Diesel made. The Diesel erupting in the hold of the boat. The sound, the smoke, the sight of the water I trailed was like seeing a finished canvas being torn by the blade of a knife. I would have to tolerate that, tolerate also the hideous sound of the Diesel. Be reasonable. That is part of it. If that sound stops then it's all over for me. To have to sit in the harbor for two or three more days would be impossible. I wish I had Melissa with me, instead of this goddamn imperative to fish.

This will be the last day, if today there is nothing.

If today there is nothing, there will be enough fuel to get this boat back to the mainland and to a broker. Just no other options, no other possibilities. Except for one. Pull the traps.

But ... the sound of the Diesel. The grotesque sound invading this ocean. The battery was charging. That was good. If the boat stopped now, I doubt if there is enough power in the battery to start it again. I don't want to, I can't, risk blowing myself up again, like I did this morning. And while the battery is charging, I can turn on the radio. I could do that from the bridge, speakers topside. Something to muffle the sound of the Diesel. The first trap not for another half an hour. I turned on the radio.

A mannequin voiced opinions and filled in space, and I was vaguely distracted. But then he put on a record, and I was not distracted, I was absorbed!

An angel's voice.

My god is that lovely. It is lovely, but pull the traps.

Pull the traps.

Joni Mitchell.

She started singing, "If you're drivin' to town with a dark cloud above you, dial in the number who's bound to love you … ."

It was taking me. I wanted it. And then the Diesel saying no, no you can't have that. No, you can't hear that. Pull the traps.

The percussioning Diesel intensified, and the churning of the Diesel became a grindstone and the knife that was sharpened by the stone was grinding into the record, making static that sounded just like knife grinding into the record as it turned, the knife tearing into her song like this boat tearing itself over the water.

The knife, at her throat!

The static that the Diesel fanned like fire.

A fire trying to catch up to her voice, and her singing against a background of flames as she tried to escape the fire like Joan of Arc.

The static.

Pull the traps.

The Diesel engine.

Pull the traps.

Destroying everything.

One or two good days.

The pistons screaming like pain that does not escape.

The pistons pounding like soldiers at doors late at night, or like nightmares invading my dreams, or wakefulness invading my sleep.

Not satisfied to strangle the silence. Not satisfied to infiltrate *me* with its horror. It was after her voice now, the angel's voice!

It was *raping* her voice.

It was raping her and I, I stood by helplessly at the wheel.

Pull my traps, I thought, my incantation.

When the day is long. My incantation. Pull the traps.

When Melissa has nothing for me. Pull the traps.

Repeat it so you hear nothing else, repeat it to the rhythm of the pistons. Pull the traps. If you shut everything else out, you will pull the traps. Shut it out for a day and when the day ends, I can return to the harbor with fish. Shut it out.

Shut everything out. Pull the traps.

"… I'm a wild flower, waiting for you …" The song.

Do it today and the pattern will be set. Then you can do it tomorrow. Pull the traps and shut everything else out. Pull them.

"But," I pleaded with myself, "the voice, the angel's voice?"

The Diesel.

Pistons beating her.

Pull the traps.

The Diesel. No.

No! I cannot do that! It was descending upon her, the Diesel! It was pulling the gentleness from her, jutting its vulgar hands down her throat. It was beating her mercilessly with the sound of the pistons. It was an attack!

Pull the traps.

"NO!" I screamed, and gulls scattered.

I raised my right hand above me, not knowing what to strike, or where, but my hand came down to the kill switch like a sword, and instantly the Diesel died, beheaded, and there was only the woman who kept on singing.

Freed.

It came from the East and filled me like sun, and the sun was just then casting rays upon the sea and sky and the cliffs that stood before me as witnesses to what had occurred, to what I had done.

I held the wheel, meaninglessly. I felt weak, and the weakness lowered me to my knees, slowly, like a man about to pray, and I was still holding the wheel, on my knees and the wheel to my breast, and the voice of the angel filling me, soothing me.

I laid myself down sobbing without tears, laid there on my back as I melted.

When my eyes were not closed, there was only the blue sky. There was the gentle rocking of the woman's voice, the gentle rocking of my body, the gentle, pelvic motion of the boat.

And then my eyes opened wildly for a moment and I realized something was happening in my hips.

My eyes closed again, softly, and I just surrendered myself to it. The woman's voice, flowing around me, into me.

I breathed not a breath of air; I breathed only of the voice and of the song. Melissa.

Gliding down my body, the hands of the voice. Making little rivers on my skin to float away all pain, cleansing me.

I felt warmth entering my shoulders, and it unfolded itself, covering me, like wings. The gentle rocking of the boat, and the voice.

And then ... then the warmth gathered itself together in my hips like the warmth of the sky gathers itself together in the sun, and my muscles contracted and breathed together, one breath, as one being, and I felt whole, and the harmonica that ushered in her voice gingerly lifted her from me and carried her away.

My hand reached up and turned off the radio. More than that I could not move, nor did I want to.

I was sobbing and now tears fell all around me.

All around me. I do not understand all this, any of this. A half an hour passed, not more, surely.

I lifted myself. I almost stood. From my knees I pulled myself to the wheel and peered over the pulpit. Before me an ocean and sky perfectly partnered. I slumped back, momentarily. My head fell into my knees, and vaguely I could feel the little knot in my back returning. I knew that the madness would begin again, when I stood, but … I stood.

I took the wheel again.

—ʌʌ— TWELVE —ʌʌ—

A sailboat would be such a nice thing to have, I thought. I brushed the helm once or twice with my hand, and I reached, sadly, for the instrument panel.

My face, for a moment, existed without eyes. It was not a question of whether they were open or not, they just did not exist. I saw nothing, and all my senses were resigned, all but the touch of my right hand, as it navigated the panel of inaccurate instruments, like an ant, and found the starter switch.

I depressed the switch.

Nothing.

The battery, empty.

Light and forms assimilated themselves before me and I had sight again. I could see the West End directly ahead of me, taunting me. I wish that it were storming. It was agonizingly flat.

The bridge, the helm that was no longer a bridge, was now only a watchtower. It was not more than a few miles away, the West End. Some of its features were even distinct, the features that I had used as markers by which to set and locate my traps.

Yet, they would become less distinct with the day, as I was now drifting out to sea. Imperceptibly, at first, slower than the rate at which I would drift through this day, this perfect day.

Gulls abandoned me.

Water was clear and blue around me, and deep. I was only a

few hundred yards from shore. I looked again at the starter switch. Looking for a clue. I pressed it again.

A low murmur, but nothing upon which to base even the slightest amount of hope. I looked behind me, tortuously, to the deck below, the deck that was to be filled with lobsters and activity and dripping with kelp and salt water.

I looked at the hatch, the coffin lid under which was a Gray Marine engine. I stepped down to the decks, mumbling vague soliloquies, and I walked to the bow, and I inhaled the first feather-puffs of breeze, as it discovered my boat.

I thought of a time I, no, we, Melissa and I were swimming, and a seal pup discovered us. It swam between us and around us and spun summersaults, and all in fun, inviting us to play, all in fun and innocence. The breeze swirled around me now lightly in the same way. It was a seal discovering a peculiar sea-creature. Without fear, it engaged us. Without fear, I marveled at its freedom. Strange. The breeze did not even seem remotely related to the wind as I had come to know it. I just could not make that association. I smiled, as I thought of the seal.

I walked back to the stern deck, and my fingers hooked the rusted rung of the engine hatch, and I slid it back, and the heat of the engine ascended into me. I was starting to understand what had happened.

Not enough oil. I had run the boat too fast. It had made the pistons swell in the chambers, and that created all the clatter. As long as the engine was running, and the oil, what there was of it, was flowing, the pistons could perform. But, when I stopped the engine the libido was lost, and the oil drained before the pistons could cool, and they were swelling, seized in the chambers, and the battery was not strong enough to get them moving again. If the battery were stronger, it might have started. I could only wait, now, as the pistons cooled and contracted and could be more easily started with a weak battery.

I went below to fix a cup of coffee. That's right. I had forgotten, the valve being broken. Alcohol in the stove, but the valve filled with rust, functionless. I drank water.

I went back and I looked into the pit. The Gray Marine engine was on its haunches. Water and oil sloshed under it, bilge water. A rogue elephant sloshing in its own excretions in a noonday sun.

I took my shirt, my rag, and wiped oil from it, the spattering from the bilge. That accomplished nothing. Again were my nostrils filled with the scent of Diesel fuel, till they could hold nothing else.

The music, the voice, had been so lovely.

I went up to the helm again, and it was an act that had no meaning, as the helm had no meaning, powerless thing that it was. I spun the wheel.

I wish it were the wheel of a sailboat. I wish it were the wheel of a sailboat, finding little lee shores and beaches and coves. Fall asleep in the sun. Like the people who came down from San Francisco. Five days down to here. They looked strong, but they were hungry. God, we fed them well, the night they tied alongside us.

And their little boy. Confident as hell. Not more than three years old. Climbed right up on my lap and played with my beard. Climbed up while Melissa was at the table, and sat on her lap. Opened her shirt to look at her breasts, to feel them, and then turned to smile at his own mother when he found them. Smiled at Melissa, too. Climbed all over the boat, inspecting everything, and then he and his father and I went up on the bridge and we could see the whole harbor, and the opening that led to the Pacific. I told him what he wanted to know about navigation from here to San Diego. He told me what I wanted to know about his week at sea, and his little boy held the wheel, making his own adventure. God, it was good that we had taken in a lot of lobsters that day.

Why, in December, how in December, a sun such as this? It was full and generous and the cliffs looked clean and noble and even the water sparkled. Just a few days more and there will be no trace of the storm, the water even by the fringe of the island blue again. A little more rough weather, perhaps, but progressively getting better.

Like bread, though, the day staled, all the while as I drifted. Spinning over the water like a leaf on a pond. And then the sun seemed to be so distant, and so disinterested in me.

The boat lolled in the troughs of the swells and the tongue beat itself hopelessly against the ship's bell, and the sound seemed to awaken the wind. One o'clock in the afternoon, perhaps, without a thing to show for it, or a rationale to explain away why there is not a thing to show for it. I gauged by the hour and by my distance from the island that I would be running home in the trough as opposed to into the wind or with the swells.

The boat hanging on the ocean like a sail to a mast in a windless air. I feel so old. I feel like I am a refugee from youth cast out before my time, and all my words and ideas are hanging from my old arms like overworked muscles that have long contemplated mutiny. I feel like a refugee from myself, not knowing where to immigrate, or how, and I steal across my own border lines to escape persecution and tortures.

I went to the hatch cover again, to look once more at the face of the Gray Marine engine. The hatch was like the window in the cabin, I looked through it into that which dwarfed me. The odor and the heat still ascended, though milder, but I decided to wait a few more hours. I would be draining the battery in my attempts to start the boat, a few more hours adrift and it will surely be cool enough to start.

And, of course, I would rather steal in with darkness.

I entered the cabin again, and crawled up to the bunk, and I hid there, disguising myself with sleep, as if to avoid being discovered by my own inadequacy. My body, carrying about forty hours of wakefulness conspired with me, helped me in my mock escape. I slept until the sloshing of the water in the bilge awakened me, the sloshing that comes only when the wind picks up, the wind that picks up only when the hour is late, the hour getting late to cooperate with the incurring darkness.

I came to the deck to see the sun evaporate, to see Catalina in the distance. If the engine did not start this time … A storm, by morning, I think. The sky making such a prediction credible, in spite of the fact that it had been so clear earlier. I had enough power in the battery to get a radio call out, I think. But, if I do that, surely there will not be enough juice to get the engine turning.

For a moment I thought that perhaps the radio call would be best. I would surely have enough for that, enough power in the battery. But in my sleep, a plan had come to me. It was not my plan, I am not the guilty one. It came to me while I was sleeping, honestly.

To be pulled in by another boat was not a part of the plan.

I palmed the engine, which was of course cooled. To out-distance the impending fear, I mounted the cabin as quickly as I could, and I depressed the starter switch.

There was grunting and discomfort, yet the engine begrudgingly obeyed, and was turning.

I took the helm and redirected the bow towards the island, towards the droop in the island that I knew to be the Isthmus, Cat Head. The sky became blue, the dark blue that soon becomes black. The boat rocked in the trough, like a woman rocks who is wailing, and I was tossed from swell to swell, like a collection plate passed from hand to hand, and the bell ringing and pulsating around the boat like a heartbeat, and a longing for the harbor. The harbor.

I remembered when my father died, but I don't know why I am thinking about death. I was living in another city, and I got a telegram … .

The engine kept turning.

"I want a fucking son!" I shouted, and the boat just kept rocking in sorrow, and the bell leading the mourners, and the harbor, an hour deeper into the darkness and the distance … Melissa, I want a son … .

Not much conversation these days. A son would change that. But, my interest in you, yours in me, is that nothing more than vaseline, just to get us moist? To help us want a child? I want a son.

And when my father died, I looked at Melissa, and I fell to my knees before her, and I began to pull her clothes down and I was sobbing.

"I will not be used that way!" she said, but I needed her so bad. He was dead and the first thing that I wanted was to be in her, and I felt her legs stiffen as I tried to pull the faded jeans from her, "I will not!" she said, and how disgusting that I could actually think of doing it on the day my father died, she said. How immoral. "I want a fucking son!" I cried again. The island and the harbor dark before me, and the island looking soft and inviting. The moon, the moon which had always been there, began to shine as the darkness intensified.

The moon, like a tiara on the forehead of a dark-skinned woman. Lovely, on the dark skin, the sky cloudless, cloudless but for a small cloud in the corner of the sky.

So lovely, this moon, brilliant on the soft dark skin and so lovely, and the small cloud stole its way across the sky, camouflaged against a starless-ness, and the moon before me, so lovely.

And then the cloud, it took the tiara in its fist, and the bow of the boat turned dark and even the sea became invisible—took the moon in its fist and stole it, and ran off with it and it was simply gone, and there was only the sound of the Diesel and the bell. That's all that was left and the silver flames on the black water disappeared. And yet the harbor and the island were before me, the lights from the mainland making the Island somehow distinct.

"I want a *son!*" I screamed.

No, I don't.

I want again to be a little boy.

The boat pulsating desperately, rocking in the troughs, and Cat Head, closer and closer. Melissa.

The harbor, I was no longer crying, and knew that I would never cry again. It had out-served its purpose. The ones who flip their cigarettes, who feign indifference to the women who just can't help themselves and want to run a comb through their hair and persuade them to slow down on their drinking—what makes them shed a tear?

The harbor, to take me in, and away from all this. Melissa, to take me in and she would have, if she understood. She just didn't understand, that's all. Just the harbor. And when he died, that day, she did not understand, and she turned me away, but the harbor will not.

The harbor before me, in the cool darkness. The sky vacant and the moon lost and the sea cold and hostile, and I leaned forward as if to bring it closer and sooner to me.

Yes. Cat Head. Santa Catalina Island. The harbor.

The harbor opened up for me, like the hips of the woman I have betrayed, and pulled me in from the night and my aloneness. I grasped the mooring line, as if for breath.

─ৠ─ THIRTEEN ─ৠ─

The glow from the lights of L.A. was suspended softly in the night air over the settlement at the Isthmus like a halo, and the breeze was no more than breath, and of a silent nature, unhurried, and seaward bound, as was I, for the boat lay moored between the landing and the harbor mouth.

The other boats, huddled once again in sleep, and my boat, the old Monterey boat, alone, sleeping.

Tonight, I too shall sleep alone. I … I pondered the absurdity of the thought. I will not sleep at all, tonight, no doubt. Sleep, my anesthetic. Tonight, not. Tonight, nothing for the pain.

I had met Melissa on shore at the Isthmus, and it was then that the lies began. "I will be up all night," I said. "I have work to do on the boat," I said. "You need a good night's sleep," I said, "and can't get that if I am working." I needed to dismantle and clear the fuel lines, I told her. "I was well on my way to The West End, and the Diesel just died." And so on. She obeyed, and perhaps even believed. She would spend the night with the woman who ran the small cafe.

"So much to do," I said, and yet, I had walked several hours alone away from all that I had to do. A few days, just a couple of good days would have made such a difference.

When I could bear the wandering no longer, could tolerate my weakness no longer, I was at last drawn to my task, that which I had resigned myself to do.

I just hope that she hasn't had the restlessness to walk, or at least, if she had the restlessness, I hope that it was weakened by her weariness, for if she has walked by this way and has seen the boat so dark she will not be able to lie to herself any longer. She must know that I have not told her the truth about what I am doing tonight. I hope that she is sleeping.

I hope that she does not wake.

I hope she is warm and under dry blankets and I hope it is better when she wakes up in the morning.

I thought these things in time to the gentle rhythm of the lapping of the water on the pilings of the landing. My hands, pocketed within me for a last exposure to warmth, burst daringly into the night air, and took the damp mossy cord that tethered the skiff to the landing like a pony.

I took the oar, and poled myself from the very shallow water by the landing, and when it became too deep, I sat down with my back to the bow, and used the oar in my hands over the stern like a tiller, the mild current and the mild breeze getting along with each other, each leading, though at different paces, through the irregular harbor and out to sea.

I was content with that, the slow drift. The night being soft, as if it had dimension. Even the halo seemed to be something I could touch, something a mystery, but with body, like the phosphorous that I trailed when I sculled the oar every few moments.

Dew, like that settling on my shoulders, would be settling on the boat now, cleansing away the salt that was scattered over the decks on every fresh scar. But I did not think long of the boat in its misery, I could not, and to distract me was the fan-shaped aura of the Isthmus, where Melissa was sleeping.

The boat, thoughts of it at least, came drifting towards me again, and bumped me gently from thinking about Melissa. The boat, healing itself with sleep. It has taken such a beating lately, and can't recover so easily, as once it could.

The sculling of the oar on the water harmonized with the silence, reaching into the water for sad and deep chords like a hand reaches into a guitar to search out its own sad and low chords, and casts them adrift into the night. I dipped the oar lightly.

How moist and supple is the water. I mean, what is under me is so smooth and undisturbed, I am amazed that it is something so ordinary as water upon which I glide.

I dipped the oar into the water once again, and the gentle slushing became memorized, like a song. Charmed, by the sound, I dipped my hand over the rail. It was warm. Just deception, I know, with the night air being so very cold, but the water felt so warm to me … and it was smooth and moist, and of course, I thought of Melissa, of her smoothness. But then, I was not comparing them, for they seemed to be one and the same. Smooth like Melissa is smooth, moist like … moist like she used to be, moist for me.

The water cooled on my hand as I held it to the night. I took it to me, under my sweater, pinioned it there with my other arm as best I could, keeping the oar in place to guide me, and the distance being less than a few moments away. I could hear the water slapping the Monterey bat on its bow. It had swung 'round with the current and the bow was before me like a great rock in the night, or so at least it appeared to me, when I at last looked over my shoulder for a bearing.

I altered the tiller accordingly, and I began to glide past the boat, to catch it on the stern where the cleats were, where it is easiest to board. All was silent.

Like a beached whale, almost, the boat.

My hand took a stanchion as I drifted down its length. The glance of a hundred yards told me that the other fishermen were asleep, only the anchor lights showing, the ports being dark. The hour, not late, but they must sense good weather, which I did not perceive, and are sacrificing themselves to it. I get so confused, trying to anticipate the weather.

Sleeping more than they need for early starts and long days while the weather holds. I think it will storm, tomorrow, but then, they know more about it, I think. At least, they are sleeping, and it can't be without reason .

Tonight, I'll be getting out of this.

The thought fell onto me as subtly as the dew, as subtly as the whisper of destruction.

And the rhythm that was in the water and that was in the night and that was in the darkness, that was in my body, became the rhythm to which I stepped into my boat. I tied my skiff to the unsuspecting Monterey hull. This time, a very loose loop, for the night was easy and there was no strain on the line, no pulling.

That's right, I thought, no pulling.

It just flows behind the boat, so naturally, without any pulling or straining. All quite passive, as if inviting all this.

I looked across the transom, before I had boarded. Diesel smoke had buried, shrouded and buried the name of the boat. I did not wipe the soot away, perhaps I should have done so, but I was not strong enough. Anyway, if I must do this, it is better for me to do it to something anonymous, to help keep the memory indistinct. It remained covered.

Yet, I whispered its name, out of the hope that the sound could voyage out into the night, away from this place, out of this harbor, sailing to those lights, the stars that sometimes appeared from behind the fog like beacons to guide it from here, and I wished that it could carry me with it but as I made the wish …

… the sound was gone, and was echoless.

The name that I had whispered was gone, departing like a ship, its running lights visible but distant, then, gone.

I found myself on the deck, the small skiff trailing behind. The glow over the Isthmus, the lights from the other boats, vanishing from time to time, a fog developing.

That is good, too, 1 suppose, for things like this.

There was a very subtle motion to the boat, like that which

accompanies the breathing of sleep. I did not wish to disturb that. I had respect for things like that. The helm was before me, above me, like a pulpit from which I could preach to the open but empty sea. My hand instinctively reached for the ladder, but I did not ascend. I wanted to very badly, but, to stand on the bridge, to look once again at the bow of my boat and the water beneath it, would start it all over again, the dream and believing in it. I slipped my hand once or twice up the length of the ladder, before taking the cool brass handle of the hatchway.

The wood swelling under the paint formed distinct vertical ridges on the hatch where the planks dove-tailed together, and the paint had held there as precariously as the shale on the escarpments on the windward side of the island.

I eased the hatch open soundlessly, and my hand slipped from the smooth moist handle and I lowered myself inside, pulling the door behind me like I might pull a cape over my shoulders on a damp night such as this.

Colors were non-existent within the cabin. There was only the dull gray, like the feathers of a gull that makes it invisible against the sea or overcast sky. But, of course, I had no trouble locating the corner, into which I filled like tide, and waited for my eyes to adapt themselves.

The darkness intensified, like fingers become a fist and I stayed in the shadow as light dripped in through the salted ports, and filled the table like a tide pool is filled, and then it even overflowed, and the light from the moon was spilling over the edges, a fountain. The moon had been returned.

The dull silver glow was the only color in the room now, but I could see silhouettes of other objects in the room, and on the table.

One of them, I observed, was my hand.

It began sliding, tacking its way across the table like a sailboat in almost no breeze. At times, for moments or even longer, my hand was motionless, becalmed, and I found myself being distracted by the faint sounds of the night, but when I look again on the table, I could see that my hand had moved, was moving, was taking wind, and progressing along the table.

Intermittently, the ocean dried up, the light evaporated as the fog journeyed past the window. I pressed my cheek against the port. The window was cold and moist. I looked down on the table again. When the light became better, my hand would move. That's right. There must be some relationship between wind and light, for the currents of air change with the day and night. My hand cruised again. I was spellbound to see how autonomous it had become.

Then my hand became a hand again, and it was telling me things about the table, searching out flaws but finding no imperfections. It was such a smooth table, like the harbor water this evening. It disappeared behind the shadow of a wine bottle, but soon it was making its own shadow again. A bit further to the edge, it found my watch cap, drifted up against it, but with the same gentleness that seemed to be in me, and the night.

I could see that the curtain was drawn, and I wanted to pull it open, to look behind it at my bed, to help me imagine to myself how good it would be to sleep, how good to lie down, and to have Melissa with me. To have Melissa with me.

I looked at my hand, to see if it could be a willing partner for a stray desire that I had, but it was too late, for it had discovered the box of matches on some obscure part of the table.

Slowly, it took the matches to within its dominion, like an eddy captures flotsam, and spins it in small circles. The matches were within my control now, and accordingly, my thoughts became more precise.

My imagination searched one last time for alternatives. A few good days of fishing would certainly have provided a few more possibilities, but alternatives are only obstacles to the inevitable, and eventually are overcome, must be overcome.

Mine were.

There was only a right hand, which was no longer mine, and the matches that were now open in a box before it.

A co-conspirator appeared from the east, like a sister ship. My left hand. It was on the table now, and its course was direct, as if well planned, as if also the wind were in its favor. Straight to the wine bottle and candle.

That too, like so many things this evening is strange. I have always called it a wine bottle. It isn't really. Melissa called it that too. It's just a ketchup bottle. Not even green. But it's strange. In order to perpetuate our belief that it is a wine bottle, one of us, I don't remember which of us, cleaned off the table, the most striking evidence that it is only a ketchup bottle. With the wax running down it, it looks like it should be a wine bottle, with a Portuguese label, or something. It's too humble an alter for the candle.

The candle on the wine bottle had melted down and was just a stub. It seemed co-operative to this. I had been gazing through the glass again, and could see nothing of the fishing boats, I could not even see the island. But when I looked again before me, the candle stub was detached and on the table, leaving the bottle uncorked, and my hands were resting listlessly, as if on a mooring.

I began to fill with fear, but not like a sail fills itself, not anything as potent or as driving. It is more like a body that fills with old age. And, in the confines of my fear, there was a longing that was not clear, and yet, I swear I could hear Melissa breathing softly, as if to give my longing a name. I have been giving her my emptiness, but a few good days of talking will change all that, just a few good days.

Melissa, it is something that must be done, though god knows, by what imperative. Surely I can find an explanation when I am finished, and if you can share that rationale with me it will certainly be convenient.

This ocean, this fishing that we put it through, is just torturing it. I can kill it. I can kill this thing that is murdering us. Anyway, death is certainly not an end to living, death is an end to dying and this boat was broken long ago. I hear it straining in the night, moaning and swelling and twisting and working so hard to die. The Diesel, even the Diesel throbs unwillingly these days. It has drifted past its former self, this boat, and can never be a salmon boat again, never up north taking the rolling seas for which it was made. Living and cruising on this flat sea is against its whole nature, an insult to its design. And besides, it's so old. Built in the Thirties, I think. Somehow that makes it less a sin to do it. It's so dangerous. I fear for myself, sometimes, while I'm on it.

Even while we are sleeping. These planks must have worms and ...

Overkill ... .

I dropped it.

Rationales and trying to make them fit what was happening, trying desperately for some coherency, but it just wasn't there. To argue now is dangerous, for an argument can be lost and if it is lost, it is not yet over for me, not yet broken, the circumstances that keep me this way. I will always be just a few good days behind in the fishing, while the boat gets deeper and deeper in need. Do it now, while you've got it in your hands, especially now, while it is dark, and a fog will accommodate you, obscure you.

I took the stub and replaced it on top of the ketchup bottle. I rubbed it in carefully. I held it up to the light of the moon like a voice. Enough. Yes, that should be enough. If I had filled it, there would be no room for the vapors, and of course, it is the vapors that are most volatile. Half full, about.

I closed my eyes, recalling and memorizing the act of tapping the alcohol from the stove, and draining it into the bottle. I want to be certain that it is I who do this, and not just some imposter that I have dream-created.

Yes, they are my hands, and I do this thing.

Three, maybe four matches, all the same fate, and I dropped them to the table, one of them still flaming, and they formed a black skeleton on a grey, a silver grey surface.

Perhaps, more of a fisherman than I thought. My hands so insulated that fire could not even break through. And if this is what is happening to my body, what can possibly he happening to my soul, which I have never touched, but only felt? I closed my eyes. I squeezed them like a wine press. Dry. Nothing.

I thought of pain. Pain was only a thought, for I had become insulated to it. Pain, I thought then only about pain, like a memory. Slowly, like sand drying on the beach, my insulation began to wear off, and pain filled the void, entering my thumb and forefinger and they began to throb with the burning of the fire. And I tried to shake off the pain, like I had shaken the flame off the first match into the darkness, but it would not leave and I sucked it, trying to swallow it but it clung to me, clung to me and I knew it was real, and I knew who I was and that it was truly I who had done the thing with the matches, and that it would be I who would do the thing to the boat.

If I strike another match, I can anticipate that it will hurt, I have broken through that barrier. Pain seemed to travel down my arm and collect in my fingers, instead of coming from some external source or power or will. It collected like blood cauterizing.

I took another match, and held this one in my palm before I could take it between my swelling thumb and forefinger. This was fire I held in my hand, this was pain looking for an escape, looking for release. Tonight, I shall release it, I too shall be released. I skewered the blister that had formed on my fingers, and I saw the substance of my pain, could feel it evaporating on my skin, escaping into the night.

Intuitively, I knew that the match that was in my hand would be the last.

I opened up the darkness once more, and I passed the knowledge of light and fire from the wood to the candle, the small unsuspecting stub that was the only obstruction now between what I imagined myself doing, and my imagination's fruit. An inch of wax, not even that, to break through and then it would be over. I had reduced the candle to nothing more than a fuse.

I watched the first few beadlets of wax spill, dripping down the candle on the bottle. I watched and listened to it breathe, listened to it swell with breath as I swelled with breath, and the match expired … but the candle was still burning, pulling the wick from the wax, like a trap, like me pulling a trap, peeling down the wax.

And I started crying. I thought I was done with that.

I stayed a few minutes longer, my breath, my chest, trying to gather the wind to blow it out, trying so hard to blow it out. I don't know what was keeping me alive, I couldn't seem to breathe, I seemed to be choking in the stale cabin and my tears were melting down my face and the sad candle pulling itself deeper into the night and destruction.

I couldn't take it anymore, and the candle was so short now. I was trembling and I took to the hatch, and I was out of the cabin and on the deck. And I shut the door so softly but I put my whole weight into it, and sealed it tight, and I looked through the stern port. I looked once, to see it shining there, alive and shining by my hand, but then I shriveled away from the window, as an image of flying glass crossed my mind and I pulled my hands to my face and fell down to my knees. I staggered, crawling, stumbling, weak and nauseous, I staggered to the stern and I untied the skiff, and I delivered myself into it, I looked back again and could see a glow and it surged again, the sadness, and I undid the skiff, and cast myself away from my deed. Done now.

My legs, uncertain and trembling. Traitorously, I fell again to my knees and the skiff quivered with me. I took the oar, fear now, I know what fire can do, I started to paddle myself from it and the lines of the boat were at once indistinct, my eyes glassed over with tears, and the fog so thick, and I shivered, I shivered and my fear drove me to words, and I started to sing out loud but so weakly,

"*Put a candle in my window,*
And I feel I got to move."

And whimpered more of the song:

"*Though I'm goin', goin',*
you don't have to worry, no no,
long as I, can see the light."

And then silence swelled in me, looking for some way to break out. "No, I can't," I said it aloud, "I can't," and I turned, to get back to the boat, to find the breath, to smother the flame, to send it off into the night, as it had sent me off into the night. I can't, I can't.

And then I fell weak to the side of the skiff, damn, I am rowing so slowly! If only I had two oars, just a few good days of fishing would have changed all that, just a few good days, and I fell to the frame of the skiff and knew it was too late, knew it was done, and I was all alone.

And then silence fell on the night and the boat and on me and on everything else, and I knew, I knew it was time. I looked, fifty yards from me now, and could somehow see a dull light in the glass from the stern, the flame nursing on the wick.

Then the explosion.

The sound was more than I could have ever imagined, pain and disbelief, and the glass shattered and I held my face again, and then looked back to see the flames escaping through the broken windows, and the whole cabin top was ablaze and I buried my head and begged for blindness, but my sight was drawn to the fire again, the fire clawing at the night trying so hard to escape, pulling its way into the darkness, and then out of the darkness, while sinking, scrambling up against non-existent walls, trying to climb out of itself, but falling back down into itself, flame consuming itself.

And then, within me, fire! Deep within me, in my chest or far deeper, flame.

A scream exploded, erupted within me.

It burst through the flu of my throat, slashing, tearing, and burning as it escaped, and burning my lungs within me. And I became lost to it, and it intensified, and I was helpless against it.

I pulled my hands over my mouth, to suffocate the fire within me and my eyes watered and blistered from the heat, and I felt myself choking on the tasteless smoke of my extinguished scream. I dropped my hands to breathe again, and the first breath of air revived the flame in me, and I screamed again, breathing out the fire that had no color.

The flame on the boat, looking for some foothold to escape, screaming all the while like me and finding no relief, and then the horror that this was really happening, and the flame from the cabin not more than a minute old, found the Diesel fuel and the flame in one last desperate panic exploded again, and this time the fire climbed higher, and the sound became more monstrous and it seemed to try every corner of the harbor, looking for a way out and finding the only out was up, scrambling over its own flames, its own fire, higher and higher into the night and the darkness, and the fog scattered in panic from around the walls of the flame, and I in panic dropped into the bottom of the skiff, contorting, as if to escape my own burning self, and ashes started to fall, and I could hear the cinders hissing all around me, and smoke rising from scattered spars that had been wretched free by the explosion of the fuel drums, and cast down in frustration and panic and left to burn, and smoke and fog was breathing on me as I lay doubled over in the dory, and I kneeled again up to the rail and the flame was still there calling me, calling out my name, *murderer!*

And from within me a deep feeling again, like I was going to be attacked by another flame but this time it was not flame, rushing up from within me, and my body knotted and I vomited over the side, and then in my weakness fell over backwards, and vomited on myself and into the skiff.

I heaved myself dry, but still knotted over my body contorted and there was nothing. My throat was swollen and throbbing, and my brow was pounding from within, like someone inside me who did not escape trying futility to thrust his way out into the night and away from all this. God away from all this!

I was on my back, lying in the salt water on the bottom of the skiff, the sky above me was throbbing red and orange, and was spackled with red cinders that trailed black smoke to mark where they were falling, like a siege of falling stars.

I looked; I summoned myself once more to the rail, and I peered over the edge and I watched the skeletal boat go down, pulling the flame with it, drowning, drowning, burning, drowning, dead, dying, dead, under, gone. And then just smoke.

The sounds of other boats starting up, and my sobbing, and darkness.

Darkness, visual silence, smuggled me away and I disappeared into the smell of the smoke, and the fog, and the outgoing tide.

I pulled thoughts of Melissa over me, like a heat shield. Melissa, my incantation. Melissa. Things, not quite as they should be between us, but a few good days of talking things over should change all that. Just a few good days.

About the Author

Thornton Sully has Jack Londoned his way across the globe sleeping with whatever country would have him, and picking up stray stories along the way. A litter of dog-eared passports that have taken up residence in his sock drawer are a constant temptation.

A Word with You Press

Publishers and Purveyors of Fine Stories in the Digital Age

In addition to being a full-service publishing house founded in 2009, A Word with You Press is a playful, passionate, and prolific consortium of writers connected by our collective love of the written word. We are, as well, devoted readers drawn to the notion that there is nothing more beautiful or powerful than a well-told story.

We realize that great writers and artists don't just happen. They are created by nurturing, mentoring, and by inspiration. We provide this literary triad through our interactive website, www. awordwithyoupress.com.

Visit us here to enter our writing contests and to become part of a broad but highly personal writing community. Improve your skills with what has become a significant, de facto writers' workshop, and approach us with your own publishing dreams and ambitions. We are always looking for new talent. Visit our store to buy from a distinguished list of our books, which include the work of a Pulitzer Prize winner, an award-winning poet, and first-rate literary fiction. Attend our seminars and retreats, and consider joining our growing list of published authors.

A writer is among the lucky few who discovers that art is not a diversion or distraction from everyday life; rather, art is an essential expression of the human spirit.

If you are such a writer, join us on our website, www. awordwithyoupress.com. If you have a project to discuss, we will assess the first thirty pages you send us pro-bono. Send your inquiries to the Editor-in-Chief, Thornton Sully, at thorn@awordwithyoupress. com. Be sure to indicate in the subject line "pro-bono assessment" and send your submission as a word doc attachment.

Angus MacDream and the Roktopus Rogue
by Isabelle Freedman

Young adults on a mythical Scottish island save the
world. Delightfully illustrated by Teri Rider.

The Wanderer
by Derek Thompson

A stranger wakes up on a deserted beach and embarks on a
journey of discovery. The first in our *Magical Realism* series.

***The Coffee Shop Chronicles, Vol. I,
Oh, the Places I Have Bean!***

An anthology of award-winning stories inspired by
events that occurred over a cup of coffee.

***The Coffee Shop Chronicles, Vol. II,
A Jolt of Espresso***

Stories condensed to exactly 100 words each,
inspired by our favorite brew.

Visiting Angels and Home Devils
by Dr. Don Hanley, Ph.D.

A discussion guide for couples.

The Courtesans of God
by Thornton Sully

A novel based on the real life of a temple priestess
in the palace of the King of Malaysia.

Bounce
by Pulitzer Prize winner Jonathan Freedman

A nutty watermelon man, a spurned she-lawyer, a
frustrated carioca journalist and a misanthropic
parrot set out to Brazil to change the world.

Left Unlatched
in the hopes that you'll come in...
A Book of Poetry by R.T. Sedgwick

Winner of the 2012 San Diego Book Awards – Poetry.

The Sky is Not the Limit
A Book of Poetry by R.T. Sedgwick

Our Award-Winning Poet follows through
with a volume of new work.

Raw Man
by Pulitzer-Prize nominee Fred Rivera, winner at
the 2015 International Latino Book Awards

This lightly-novelized Vietnam memoir, now required reading
at major universities, derives its title from the author's epiphany:
"Twenty-seven years after I got on the flight home, I saw that Nam
war was just raw man spelled backwards. I'm pretty raw today."

The Boy with a Torn Hat
by Thornton Sully

Debut novel was a finalist in the 2010 USA
Book Awards for Literary Fiction

"Henry Miller meets Bob Dylan in this coming of age romp played
out in the twisted alleyways and smoky beer halls of Heidelberg.
Sully is a cunning wordsmith and master of bringing music to
art and art to language. Excessive, expressive, lusty, and once in a
blue metaphor—profound. Here is what I mean: 'Some women are
imprisoned like a tongue in a bell—they swing violently but unnoticed until the moment of contact with the bronze perimeter of
their existence—and thenthe sound they make astonishes us its
power and pain and beauty, and its immediacy' —Wunderbar"
—Jonathan Freedman, Pulitzer Prize winner

A Word with You, Vol. I
The Best from A Word with You Press

An anthology of select winners from the literary contests of *A Word with You Press* from 2009 to 2015

Max and Cheez go to Spain
by Naureen Zaim and David Ulrich

A delightful illustrated children's book finds two cats on the first of
many adventures, stowing away in a suitcase to Spain. What other
countries will they investigate, now that they have the travel bug? A
great way to introduce young children to the cultures of the world.

Falling for France
by Nancy Milby

The first in *A Foreign Affair* series finds Annie Shaw having to choose between a successful career and real romance with a French aristocrat, and wanting both.

French Twist
by Nancy Milby

The saga continues as American archeologist Louise Marcel becomes entangled in nasty business on French soil, as she conceals her own hidden agenda.

Finding France
by Nancy Milby

The third in *A Foreign Affair* series finds Gabrielle Walker lamenting a life unraveling when a letter informs her she is the inheritor of a large estate in France. Then it gets complicated!

Finding Home
by Nancy Milby

Etienne, the recurring enigma in the series *A Foreign Affair*, is brutal to his enemies but a gentle giant to those he loves. Can the secret woman in his past enter his life again? Perhaps, but not with complications—some predictable, but some …

Visit our on-line store at www.awordwithyoupress.com. Most books are available as print editions and ebooks. We have also a growing selection of gifts for writers, and please check out our latest contests! We'd love a word from you!

A Word with You Press
Publishers and Purveyors of Fine Stories in the Digital Age
310 East A Street
Suite B
Moscow, Idaho 83843

Made in the USA
Middletown, DE
07 November 2021

51766294R00083